# TROUBLE ABOARD SHIP

Working as quietly as possible, Cord pried the top off the barrel. Then he stuffed all but one of the dynamite sticks inside, burying them under a mass of ten-penny nails. Finally he lit the last stick from a burning timber, shoved it into the nails, and replaced the barrel lid.

"What you doing, mister?" asked a gruff voice.

Cord didn't hesitate. He sent a screaming .45 caliber shell into the moist tissues of his frontal lobes. The looter was still dying when Cord broadjumped him and rolled behind the stacked wine barrels.

Six looters rushed in, guns blazing. The dynamite blew them into ground beef.

Cord Diamondback was unhurt. After a minute he sat up and shook his head, groaning.

That's when he felt the twin barrels of a shotgun pressed against the small of his back.

*Also in the DIAMONDBACK series from Pinnacle Books*

# DIAMONDBACK

#9

## POISON BAY

### PIKE BISHOP

PINNACLE BOOKS          NEW YORK

DIAMONDBACK #9: POISON BAY

*Copyright © 1985 by Raymond Obstfeld*

An original Pinnacle Books edition, published for the first time anywhere.

First printing/October 1985

ISBN: 0-523-42288-1
Can. ISBN: 0-523-43292-5

*Printed in the United States of America*

PINNACLE BOOKS, INC.
1430 Broadway
New York, New York 10018

9    8    7    6    5    4    3    2    1

*To J. B. Allen,*
*the meanest cuss ever to wield a word processor*

# POISON BAY

# 1

---

"Something's wrong," said Cord Diamondback, leaning out over the railing of the *Brandywine Princess*.

"What do you mean?" asked Kimberly Bryce, gripping his shoulder. "I don't see anything."

Cord ignored her, moving quickly along the railing, trying to get a better look through the darkness. Fog pressed in on the hurricane deck of the eighty-ton steamship, blurring his view.

"What is it, Cord?" Kimberly persisted, a little frightened now.

Cord pointed to starboard. "Over there."

Kimberly squinted hard. At first she saw nothing, just a murky blur of shoreline against a dark, moonless sky. She strained to listen but heard only the throbbing of the ship's engines and the rhythmic splash of the paddle wheel driving them forward.

But as her eyes adjusted to the darkness, she could see what Cord meant: a jagged line of lights, dotting the shore of the Sacramento River. The lights formed a broken line, bending slightly to starboard, like streetlights on a curving road.

"Oh, don't worry, Cord," she said, relieved. "Those are candles, put out on floats to guide us past the rock reefs. Daddy told me all about that once. He used to work on a steamer back in Missouri—"

"They're leading us off course," Cord broke in.

Kimberly raised a skeptical eyebrow. "Why do you say that?"

"I know this river, Kimberly. We're approaching Splinter Curve, just south of Bell Ridge. There's a sharp bend here to *port,* not starboard. If we follow those lights we'll break up on the rocks."

"Well, wouldn't the captain *know* that?"

"He should," said Cord. "If he knew what he was doing."

Cord began to think he'd made a mistake when he'd bought his ticket on the *Brandywine Princess.* He'd wanted to book passage on the *Clancy Longborn,* a sternwheel steamer whose captain he knew and trusted. But the *Princess* had left earlier, and Cord needed to reach San Francisco as soon as possible—so he'd taken another boat, and was starting to regret it.

"Maybe I'll have a word with the captain," he said, leaving the rail.

"Why, Cord? What's going on?"

"That's what I'll ask him."

Cord started past her. Kimberly tried to press him for details, but just then a wiry figure jumped down from a nearby packing crate and rushed over to block their way. He looked at Cord and leered at Kimberly.

"Aren't you even going to kiss her?" he asked.

Kimberly flushed at the intrusion. The eavesdropper was a grubby lad in a burlap shirt and grimy, handmade overalls, worn clear through at the knees. He looked at the show girl and grinned.

"Dammit, Jack!" cried Kimberly, grabbing the boy by his earlobe. "Can't a girl get some peace out here?"

"Not the way you've been acting," said the boy, vainly struggling to free himself. "There's not a fella on this boat you haven't made eyes at. 'Cept me, that is—and I wasn't too young by much."

"Why, you little—" Kimberly drew back to slap him, but Cord caught her arm and held it fast. Jack danced free, hooking his thumbs under his armpits, heckling the show girl.

"Give me five years," he said, snickering. "I'll show you a good time."

"I'll show you the back of my hand, you little bastard, if you get within smacking range."

Cord sighed. He'd met Kimberly Bryce hours earlier in a Sacramento saloon, during the last hand of a card game. Cord was playing a twitchy man in a bowler hat with gray-and-white whiskers. The man had bet a bag of gold nuggets, lost it, and drew his Derringer to get it back again. Cord shrugged, tossed him the bag, and left the bar.

Kimberly caught up with him outside, on the street. She'd been watching the game and was impressed with Cord's rugged build and strong, angular features. She also liked his style—especially when he'd pocketed the gold nuggets under the table and filled the bag with shell casings. Kimberly alone had seen him do it, and she'd decided then that Cord was the man to escort her to San Francisco.

Not that Cord minded the job. Kimberly was quick-witted and full of ambition, a show girl hoping to land a job in one of the big-city theater houses. She had bushy red hair and a figure Cord would match against anyone's. When she decided to tag along, Cord had no objection—but that was before her first shouting match with a ten-year-old stowaway named Jack.

"Listen, both of you," he said firmly. "I have to see

the captain. Can you keep from killing each other while I'm gone?"

"No," said Jack. Kimberly took a swipe at his head and Jack ducked away, snickering.

Cord went upstairs and made his way to the center of the ship, past the belching black mass of the smokestacks. Seeing the captain might be unwise, he reflected, since Cord *was* a wanted man—and any official contact raised the risk of capture. But if Cord's theory about their course change was correct, exposure was the least of his worries.

He stopped before a companionway, leading up to the wheelhouse. At the foot of the stairs were two beefy roustabouts, passing a cigarette between them.

"Is the captain up there?" asked Cord.

"Sure is," said the nearer man, sucking tobacco smoke into his lungs. "He's up there with the first mate, arguing about something."

"Much obliged," said Cord, starting past him. The roustabout held up his hand.

"Uh . . . we're not supposed to let you up there, sir."

"Why not?"

"Because—" He broke off as the other man shot him a warning glance. "I don't know, just because."

"It's an emergency," said Cord, edging past him. But the second crewman stood squarely at the foot of the stairs, blocking Cord's path.

"No exceptions," said the crewman. He was thick and blocky, with mottled hair and skin like shark flesh. "We got our orders. Get lost."

"I said it's an emergency."

"And I said, get lost. I mean it, fella."

Cord's reply was cut short as a curse echoed from the wheelhouse, and broken glass sprayed from one of the windows. The crewman turned to look and Cord slammed his elbow into the man's solar plexus, doubling him up with a sound like a punctured gasbag. Cord drove his knuckles into the bland face, and a bicuspid bounced across the deck.

The crewman looked down in amazement. He frowned, working his tongue into the newfound hole, and stared fixedly at his lost tooth. Cord picked a spot on his jaw and hit him hard enough to bounce him off a bulkhead.

"How about you?" Cord asked the second crewman, as the first one sagged to the deck.

"I . . . uh . . . can't let you through, sir," he said timidly.

"And if I go up anyway?"

The crewman swung halfheartedly at Cord. Cord wrapped a fist around his collar and propelled him face first into the bulkhead. The crewman slumped onto the deck, holding his nose.

"Maybe just this once," he muttered.

"Much obliged." Cord climbed the stairs to the wheelhouse, listening to a rapid stream of conversation from above.

". . . like hell you're in charge! I was driving this tub when your mother was a snot-nosed kiddy-whore, and I'll be driving it when you're worm food in a road trench, you garbage-eating vulture!"

"Times change, Captain. The *Princess* belongs in more capable hands. And don't forget, I've got the gun."

"You want to hang for mutiny, Tibbs? You want a rope chewing at your windpipe?"

"I hardly think a maritime court would—"

"We're going to crash," said Cord, stepping into the wheelhouse.

Both men turned to look at him. The captain was seated behind an immense navigator's wheel, adjusting the heading with one hand. He had ruddy features and a sparse black beard. First Mate Tibbs was taller and leaner, with close-cropped hair and a crisp, clean uniform. In Tibbs's hand was a Smith and Wesson Pocket .32, directed at the captain.

The captain spoke first.

"What the hell do you mean, mister? We're right on course."

"Not if you're following the guide floats. They're taking us into the rock reefs."

The captain turned to look outside, squinting hard into the gloom. Outside the floats cast a watery gleam through the fog, twisting sharply to starboard. The captain gasped and said, "Tibbs, he's right! How in hell did we—"

Tibbs fired twice. The captain flew off his stool, clawing at his stomach, as the front of his shirt turned red. He made a gargling sound and lay still. Tibbs turned his gun on Diamondback and said, "Your turn."

"There's something you haven't thought of," said Cord.

Tibbs cocked his weapon. "What's that?"

"Think about it. This scheme was hatched by a band of looters. They want to run the boat aground and plunder the cargo. You were paid to divert the captain's attention."

"Yeah. So what?"

"So this: once they're on board you're a dead man. You can identify them, Tibbs. Do you think they'll let you live?"

Tibbs turned pale. "They wouldn't—"

Suddenly a figure stumbled through the doorway.

Tibbs screamed and fired blindly, blowing a hole in his breastbone. Cord drew his gun and pumped two bullets into Tibbs's throat. Tibbs fell on top of the captain.

"Sorry to bother you . . . sir," said the crewman with the lost tooth, reeling drunkenly against the door frame. "This guy came up . . . before I could stop him. Wasn't . . . my fault. Didn't have to . . . shoot me."

The crewman touched his chest, looked down at his fingers. They were red and moist. "I said . . . I was sorry, sir. Didn't . . . have to . . . shoot me." He sighed, fell back through the doorway, crashed downstairs, and slammed into the deck below.

Cord dove for the wheel.

He grabbed it and heaved, putting his back into it, struggling to bring the big steamer around. The wheel was heavy and sluggish, like a hibernating grizzly, unwilling to move. Cord gritted his teeth and heaved harder, swearing. The oaken wheel resisted a moment longer, then began to turn under his hands, slowly at first, then faster. Cord was just beginning to congratulate himself when the steamer hit the rocks.

And wrenched madly sideways.

Cord slammed into the wheel. Under him the *Brandywine Princess* bucked and screeched and lurched crazily to port, spilling charts and tools and papers everywhere. Cord clung to the wheel as the massive steamer reared up on its side, toppling a map chest out the window. A kerosene lantern shattered on the deck and set fire to it.

Cord scrambled out the door and down the companionway. The once-level deck was now a sharp incline, swaying fiendishly back and forth. As Cord stumbled forward he heard shrill screams below, and the sound of gunshots and explosions. The looters were wasting no time.

He'd just gained the head of the stairs when a dynamite blast toppled one of the *Princess*'s huge loading derricks. The ship seemed to hiccup under Cord, and a column of black oil smoke stung his eyes. He threw himself forward, bouncing and rolling down the steps onto the swaying surface of the *Princess*'s hurricane deck.

Somewhere Kimberly Bryce was screaming.

Cord rubbed his eyes and plunged blindly through the smoke, guided by the screams. By the time he found her, two men were dragging her toward the companionway. Jack was trying to help her, but a third man had him in a choke hold.

Cord drew his Schofield and gave one of Kimberly's would-be abductors a .45-caliber boost into the water. The other one let go long enough for Kimberly to plant a spiked heel in his stomach. He toppled to the deck and Cord blew a hole in his skull for good measure.

The last man let go of Jack. It wasn't good idea, because Jack snatched a loose timber off the deck and smashed it into the man's face. He backed up a step and Jack swung again, at his knees this time. The man pitched sideways, hit the rail, and somersaulted over it into the brackish water below.

A bullet whined past Cord's elbow. "Get back!" he cried, scrambling for an open doorway. Kimberly scurried in behind him. Jack tried to follow them, stumbling through the smoke. He turned the wrong way and stopped short when a spray of gunfire hit him in the face. The back of his head burst open like a baked potato.

Cord felt a wave of rage overtake him, not the noisy anger of most folks, but a cold, hard *thing* down inside that could be appeased only by violent justice. The soft trappings of culture dropped away like the skin of an onion as Cord squinted through the smoke, looking for his target.

And found him.

He was crouched by the companionway, a man with a bristly mustache and a dirty red beret. He was ugly, so ugly a wanted poster could never do him justice. Cord took aim just as the killer spotted him.

Both fired.

A slug whizzed past Cord's earlobe. Cord's bullet struck the killer's gun and exploded a powder charge in one of the chambers, sparking a chain reaction that blew the gun apart and tore the killer's hand off. Screaming, he turned to run and toppled pell-mell down the stairs, trying to grab the railing with the bloody stump of his left wrist. He bled to death before he hit the lower deck.

Cord sprinted to the rail and glanced over the side. A dozen looters were boarding the steamer, shooting wildly, picking off the passengers like poachers on a chicken farm. One tried to see how many bullets he could pump into the body of a girl in a frilled satin dress.

Smoke billowed everywhere. Cord realized that the cargo hold was burning out of control. A man-shaped figure, bathed in flame, crashed through the bottom railing and hit the water with a roar of hot steam.

"Behind you!" yelled Kimberly.

Cord spun to find two looters bounding up the companionway, not six feet from him. One drew his gun but Cord shot him first, in the stomach, knocking him backward like a tenpin. The second man jumped aside, clawing at his holster. Cord realized he was out of bullets.

The other man got his gun free.

Cord grabbed the fire axe, bracketed to the wall. A bullet whanged off the axe handle. Cord yanked it loose and split the gunman's head like a piece of firewood. The gunman fell to his knees, still waving the revolver, his eyes moving in different directions. He fired sideways, three times. The left side of his face frowned as he crumpled to the deck.

Cord inspected the bodies. The axe victim was carrying a satchel; inside were four sticks of dynamite, probably to blow up these cabins after they'd been looted. Cord put the satchel over his own shoulder and hastily reloaded his gun.

"What are you doing?" asked Kimberly.

"Taking the initiative," said Cord. "I'd rather not wait for them to come up and slaughter us."

"Can I help?"

Cord smiled at her, surprised at the show girl's willingness to pitch in under the worst of circumstances. "Maybe you can," he said. "Look for survivors. Tell them we're getting off this boat, in a hurry. Good luck." He climbed over the railing and eased himself down.

The main deck was a shambles. Supplies were littered everywhere, and smoke poured from a section of the hold. Heat pressed through the deck planks like a trapped animal, trying to break free. Cord ducked behind a stack of hay bales at the sound of approaching voices.

"I say, forget the cargo, Stretch! This whole ship is burning up. Let's get the hell out of here!"

"Not till we've got all we can carry. I didn't set this thing up just to watch our profits sink into the Sacramento."

"Ain't gonna be no profits if we're all dead."

Cord stole a glance and saw two shaggy gunmen, armed to the teeth, facing away from him. Stealthily, he pressed forward. In the central loading area Cord found a pyramid of wine barrels and a crate full of live chickens. Beyond them were stacks of pine lumber, a pile of buffalo pelts—and a barrel with NAILS painted on the side.

He had an idea.

Working as quietly as possible, Cord pried the top off the barrel. Then he stuffed all but one of the dynamite sticks inside, burying them under a mass of ten-penny nails. Finally, he lit the last stick from a burning timber, shoved it into the nails, and replaced the barrel lid.

"What you doing, mister?" asked a gruff voice.

Cord didn't hesitate. He drew his gun and spun around fast, firing wildly. Bullets whined off a crate behind the looter who'd discovered him, a man with greasy hair and no front teeth. He ducked behind a feed bag and yelled, "Hey, Stretch! Someone's in here!"

Cord turned to leave, but a barrage of bullets chewed up the crates in his path. He was trapped, with only seconds before the dynamite exploded. The looter with the missing teeth started shooting from behind the feed bag.

Cord rushed him.

"Goddamn!" he cried, stunned at the recklessness of Cord's advance. In the split-second of amazement before he could fire at such a perfect target, Cord sent a screaming .45-caliber shell into the moist tissues of his frontal lobes. The looter was still dying when Cord broadjumped him and rolled behind the stacked wine barrels.

Six looters rushed in, guns blazing. The dynamite blew them into ground beef.

The first took a faceful of metal shrapnel and fell with a hole clean through his head, a hole one could look through. The second felt his chest burst open and looked down to see his own heart beating, a rapid cadence that died when he did. The third grabbed his belly and felt a rough, wet hole, like a mud crater on a rain-slick trail.

The others took much longer to die.

Cord Diamondback was unhurt, lying prone behind the stacked barrels with his hands pressed tightly to his ears. His body was covered with a fine snowfall of ash and metal flakes. After a minute he sat up and shook his head, groaning.

That's when he felt the twin barrels of a shotgun pressed against the small of his back.

# 2

"How about it, Stretch?" asked a thick, blunt voice. "You want me to just kill him?"

"Hold up a minute, Leonard," said another man. "He's the one set off the dynamite, blew up Chuck and the boys. We don't want him to die too quick, now, do we?"

Diamondback twisted around to get a look at his captors. The one called Stretch was blocky and short, with a strawberry birthmark on his cheek. He wore a flannel scarf and a wide-brimmed Stetson, tilted low over his eyes. His gun hand was missing two fingers.

The other one, Leonard, was muscular and bare-chested. He had cobalt eyes and a dirty-blond mustache, badly in need of a trim. On his chest was a tattoo that read: ADELAIDE, FOREVER YOURS.

"Let's see, now," Stretch mused. "Where do we start?"

Leonard snorted. "How about the kneecaps?"

Cord threw himself to one side as two slugs from Stretch's gun chewed up the deck planks behind him. Stretch guffawed, adjusting his aim. Cord braced himself to roll again, but it was hopeless; there was nowhere to go. Stretch thumbed back the hammer of his six-gun.

"Maybe the stomach," he said.

"Yeah, good thinkin', Stretch. Let's find out what he had for dinner tonight."

Three gunshots split the air. Stretch looked down and realized he was missing most of his left shoulder. Blood welled from the open wounds. "Hog piss," he said, and fell on his face.

Behind him, Kimberly Bryce twisted around and fired twice at Leonard. She missed. Leonard swung the shotgun around to blast her, but Cord grabbed the weapon's barrel and boosted it out of his grasp. Leonard tried to get it back and Cord smashed the walnut stock into his nose, driving a bony splinter into Leonard's cerebral cortex.

Kimberly fired again, blowing Leonard off his feet. The gunman landed on Stretch's body, clawing at his chest. His leg twitched three times, like a dog with trail fleas, then stopped.

"Nice job," said Cord. "Looks like you saved my life."

Kimberly dropped her gun and sank to the deck, trembling with reaction shock. Cord realized it was the first time she'd shot a man. He knew what she'd be going through: shock, depression, the feeling that it hadn't really happened, not there, not now, not to *me*. He wanted to talk her through it, but right now there wasn't time.

"Let's go," he said, helping her to her feet.

"I . . . I had to do it," she said hesitantly.

"Had to, and did. Can't ask for more than that." He smiled. "Where'd you get the gun?"

"From someone you killed." She shuddered. "God knows, there were plenty to pick from."

Cord glanced around. The deck was littered with bodies and body parts, drenched with blood and bile.

One man had a fistful of nails in his face, like a sopping red pincushion. Others stirred fitfully, grasping at wounds that wouldn't close.

"What'd you find upstairs?" asked Cord.

Kimberly gathered her wits with a visible effort. "Everyone's in one of the staterooms, afraid to move," she said. "Some looters are up there, too. I was lucky to avoid them."

Cord suspected that more than luck was involved; for all her hysteria, Kimberly seemed to have a remarkable knack for doing just the right thing. He took her hand and led her forward, seeking a path through the carnage.

By now the blaze was out of control, like a forest fire in the dry season. Timbers flared all around them. If it spread much farther, the *Princess* would simply disintegrate, trapping them all in its flaming ruins—and anyone left on board would either drown or be cooked like hog meat.

The trick was to round up the survivors and get them to safety, right away. But the shoreline was at least two hundred yards from where they'd hit the reef; many of the *Princess*'s passengers would be unable to swim against the Sacramento's swift, ocean-bound current.

Cord and the show girl struggled across the treacherously leaning deck surface to the main stairway. Smoke drifted down from the upper decks, and Cord began to worry about toxic fumes. If any passengers were hiding in their cabins, the smoke inhalation could kill them as surely as any looter's bullets.

Cord and Kimberly started up the companionway toward the hurricane deck. They were three steps from the top when Cord heard voices up ahead. He ducked down, signaling the show girl back, keeping to the shadows.

"Hey, Jed," someone was saying, "how much longer 'fore they're cooked in there?"

"Can't be too much," said another man, laughing hoarsely. "I think I smell roast passenger already."

Cord squinted through the smoke, trying to get his bearings. Two men stood not ten feet from the head of the stairs, both facing the other way. Beyond them was a stateroom door, riddled with bulletholes.

"Come on out, folks!" Jed yelled. "Don't worry none, I'll make it quick. Better that than to fry like a pork chop in that fancy oven of yours."

"You can go to hell," said a timid, squeaky voice from the stateroom.

"You, too, mister," said Jed, blowing another hole in the door. Someone shrieked inside, and Jed snickered.

"Who's for target practice?" he yelled. "Anyone feeling lucky?"

"I am," said Cord.

Jed whirled around just as a .45 shell carved a tunnel through his breastbone. He clutched his chest, felt the hole, said "Shit!" and died, falling backward.

The other gunman sighted on Cord, but Cord fired first. Two cartridges perforated the man's rib cage and spat out the other side. He grunted and stepped backward, still raising his gun.

Cord shot him again, in the stomach, then ducked aside as the thrice-wounded gunman shot back, missing by five feet. The gunman kept firing, coming no closer to his target until his bullets were exhausted. He reached into his pocket and pulled out a handful of fresh shells, dropping most of them in the process.

Cord shot him in the throat.

The gunman jerked under the impact, blood spurting with every pulsebeat, but still he didn't fall. He broke open his revolver and began reloading, taking no notice of anything else, like a sleepwalker lost in a dream.

He was almost finished when Cord pressed his Schofield against the bridge of the man's nose and blew a hole clean through his head. The gunman dropped his gun and shells and sat down on the deck, looking vaguely disappointed.

"Let's get the passengers out," said Cord.

He pried open the door to the stateroom and stood back as a bedraggled crowd began to emerge, many coughing and gasping for breath. In the cabin were twelve survivors, badly shaken but mostly unhurt. Cord was wondering how to get them all to safety when an explosion echoed off the port bow.

"My God! What now?" Kimberly moaned.

Cord scanned the dark horizon, backlit by the flames rising from the ruined *Princess*. A trim, sail-driven craft was coming downriver, its deck packed with crewmen. Suddenly, the cannon fired again, but it was aimed well away from them—a signal, not an attack. Cord could see a figure on deck waving a kerosene lantern.

"It's a clipper ship," said Cord, squinting at the oncoming vessel. "They're trying to help us."

"Thank God!" said Kimberly. "I was afraid we'd all either burn or drown."

Cord said nothing. He was studying the clipper's prow, where a busty, hand-carved mermaid smiled enticingly over the ship's legend. The legend was painted in bold, Gothic letters: *Aegean*. Cord felt a thrill of recognition.

"I know that boat," he said softly.

"You do?" asked Kimberly. "Will they help us?"

"Yes, of course," said Cord. He welcomed the rescue, but his worries weren't over. In fact, they might be just starting. For the *Aegean*'s captain was an old friend of Cord's, a man who knew his most terrible secret—and who, if he wanted, could have Cord dangling from the end of a hangman's rope within the hour.

# 3

"You're out of your mind!" said Kimberly indignantly. "I'm not risking my life in *that* thing!"

"Suit yourself," said Cord. "I want you to know that I'll always remember you just as you are now—no matter what the fish do to your body."

Kimberly bristled, but said nothing. She and Cord were the last ones left on the disintegrating *Princess;* the others had already slid to safety along the length of rope strung between ships by Cord and the *Aegean*'s crewmen. A lifesaver had been fitted with straps of canvas and suspended from the rope to make a breeches buoy, a clumsy but workable system of transferring passengers.

"Isn't there any other way to do this?" asked Kimberly.

Cord nodded. "Swim."

"I can't."

"Good-bye, then." Cord took the life preserver out of her hands and started climbing into it himself.

"Cord! You wouldn't just leave me here?"

Cord shrugged, and flung one leg over the rail.

"Okay, okay! I'll do it!"

Cord helped the show girl wriggle into the lifesaver, pulling the strap up firmly between her legs. Kimberly sniffed, but said nothing. Cord eased her over the rail and gave the signal to hoist away. Soon she was moving jerkily across the gulf between ships, her eyes tightly closed.

She was almost there when the *Princess*'s boiler exploded.

Superheated shrapnel flew everywhere. The steamer bucked halfway out of the water, like a spurred stallion, with a screech of buckling metal and splintered pine. The breeches buoy shuddered and collapsed.

Kimberly screamed as the life preserver swung down and crashed into the *Aegean*'s hull. The show girl's dress flopped down over her face, revealing gaudy satin pantalettes on a pair of wildly kicking legs. She was still screaming as a dozen crewmen hauled up on the ropes, dragging her ungracefully to safety. Cord saw her grab the first crewman within arm's reach and wrap herself around him for dear life.

Then the deck lurched under Cord's feet, nearly toppling him, and he realized he should get going, too. Cord vaulted up onto the rail, braced himself, and dove head first into the churning water.

The trick was to get out as far as possible. If the current caught him and forced him back into the *Princess*'s collapsing interior, he might never get out alive. His best bet was to swim straight out and try to grab the line from the breeches buoy, now foundering in the water between ships.

Cord hit the water and remembered with a jolt how cold the Sacramento really was. It was a deadly, numbing cold, the cold of snowmelt water from the High Sierras—so cold it threatened to steal the warmth he needed to keep swimming. Cord shuddered. He'd seen sailors sink quietly beneath the waves, offering no resistance, as if their spirit had been broken by the octopus-like hold of the icy water.

He choked and swallowed a freezing mouthful. The current was clawing at him, like the hand of a giant, and he realized suddenly that in the swirling tide he'd lost all sense of direction. He struggled to keep his head above water and get his bearings, but the surging water stung his eyes and he could barely stay up long enough to breathe.

His only chance was to fight the current. The current was pulling him away from the *Aegean*, so the toughest direction was the right one. But it was also the most tiring. Already his arms and legs felt like blocks of old wood—thick, weak, and lifeless.

Far away he heard someone yelling something, probably one of the *Aegean*'s crewmen. Cord couldn't hear his words, only the tone of his voice: urgent, and worried. Other voices joined in, but Cord lost track of them as a frigid wave swept over his head.

Cord thought of how easy it would be to close his eyes and relax, to surrender to the cool embrace of the sea. It was calling him—*she* was calling him—she wanted to hold him, to caress him with her cool, white fingers. He wanted to go to her, but something nagged at him—a fragment of knowledge he'd learned long ago.

What was it? It was so hard to think anymore. Cord frowned in concentration, trying desperately to remember—and suddenly he wasn't in the water anymore, he was back at Harvard, in his medical disorders class, with a group of students in a musty laboratory. They were gathered around a blue-white corpse, watching Professor Felix Goldhaven saw open its skull.

"Amazing organ, the brain," said the professor,

lifting off a section of the cranium. Under it was the grayish mass of fatty cells that until recently had done the corpse's thinking. "When the body suffers heat loss, the brain is the first thing to shut down."

Goldhaven struck a match on the skull and lit a ten-cent cigar. "If this poor bloke had smoked one of these before plunging into the water, he might have stayed alive."

Cord opened his mouth to ask something and choked on a mouthful of seawater. The laboratory was gone. He was thrashing about in the Sacramento, rapidly freezing, a living example of the professor's words.

He shuddered. He'd been about to surrender to the sea, a kind of psychic suicide. It seemed so inviting, so frighteningly sensible, that Cord wondered what other crazy things the cold might inspire. Maybe he should dive to the bottom and look for treasure. Or swim across the ocean to China. Or take the rope he found in his hand and follow it to the people on the other side.

Stupid ideas, all of them.

Cord was about to let go of the rope in disgust when someone yanked on it, hard. Angrily, he held on. He wanted to drop the rope on purpose, not have it taken from him. The other man yanked again and Cord got so mad he wanted to find the damned rope thief and wrap the thing around his neck. That would show him.

With redoubled strength Cord worked his way up the rope, hand over hand, as the thief yanked even harder. Cord would track him down and smash him. All he had to do was follow the cord. Cord, following a cord. It was the funniest thought he'd ever had. He tried to laugh and gulped a fresh mouthful of ice-cold water.

Then Cord broke through the frigid surface and filled his lungs with air. He hadn't even realized he needed some, but it felt wonderfully good to breathe. He blinked up at the gleaming hull of the *Aegean*, towering above him, and realized with a start how close he'd come to drowning.

The rope heaved again and pulled Cord clean out of the water. He lacked the strength to hold on, but the rope was tangled around his hand and elbow and held fast anyway. Cord slid up the side of the clipper, shivering in the wind, until several pairs of waiting hands dragged him aboard and a rough wool blanket was thrown over him.

Cord's consciousness began to fade, like a lantern wick without fuel. He blinked up at the darkness and saw a swarthy, red-bearded face peering down at him.

"Beefeater McGee," he whispered.

The bearded face showed recognition, and surprise. "Goddamn!" he growled. "I know this fella! Harris, get this polecat into my cabin. I want to talk to him, right away—in private."

"All right, range rat," said Beefeater McGee, straddling a chair that creaked under his weight. "I want to know what you have to say for yourself, and I want to know *now.*"

Cord looked up, instantly regretting it. His head was pounding like a gong; his tongue felt like the doormat all the rangehands wiped their feet on. He swallowed hard, and tried to think about something besides how rotten he felt.

He was sitting up on the captain's bed, in an incredibly spacious cabin. Nautical mementos lined the walls, notably the tooth of a twenty-ton whale McGee had pursued for three days in the Caribbean.

Moby, he'd called her, although she wasn't white and he wasn't all that obsessed with catching her.

Cord shook his head to clear it. He wanted to lie down and sleep for a while, but McGee's patience, never his strong suit, was exhausted. He was going to want some answers, and Cord hoped he was clear-headed enough to provide them.

"I'm waitin'," said the red-haired captain.

"What for?" asked Cord.

McGee's neck twitched. Cord had never seen a hairier man; his hair ran down his cheeks and over his chin, a bushy carpet that covered most of his body. He was half a head taller than Cord, a thick slab of a man with a punch that could split a pine tree.

Rumor had it he'd once killed a man with a friendly slap on the back. Cord and McGee had laughed over that one, but McGee had never denied it. He liked being a bit of a legend.

"Just one question," barked McGee. "Can you think of one reason I shouldn't string you up like the cold-blooded killer you are?"

Cord shrugged. "Because I don't want to die?"

"Try again, range rat."

"Okay, because you don't want to kill me. Think a minute, McGee. You know me as well as anyone. I don't kill for no reason."

"That's what I used to think. But then I heard about Billy Fallows, and how you harpooned him—*harpooned* him, for Christ's sake—and I figured maybe I was wrong about you, Chris. Maybe I was wrong the whole time."

"You weren't wrong, McGee. And it's Cord, not Chris."

"Like hell!" McGee slammed his fist into an oaken bedside table, cracking the varnished wood. "I still say you're a yellow-bellied killer. And don't give me this Cord Diamondback horseshit, neither. You're Chris Deacon, same as always, and you're wanted all over the country for what you did to Fallows. Not that I blame you for tryin' to run and hide. If I did what you did, I'd run and hide, too."

Cord crossed his arms. "You finished?"

"Huh?"

"If you're all done with your little speech, I'll tell you what really happened."

For the first time, McGee looked puzzled. "You tryin' to trick me, Chris?"

"Nope. I'm trying to explain."

"Explain what?"

Cord sighed. "You remember my brother Eric? I used to talk about him all the time on the *Quapaw*. Eric Deacon, the San Francisco lawyer. I guess I bragged about him a little more than you cared to hear."

"I remember," said McGee, smiling in spite of himself. "Sittin' there on that whaleboat in the hundred-degree heat, you always talked about that damned brother of yours and I talked about startin' my own shippin' fleet. Well, I got the fleet, Cord, not a big one, but the ships are all mine." McGee frowned. "Your brother Eric, what happened to him?"

"Dead. Murdered."

"My God! Who done it?"

"Billy Fallows."

McGee sat back in the chair, at a loss for words. The captain's silence was so unusual that Cord knew he'd made an impression. Carefully, he continued the story.

"Senator Fallows wasn't the hero everyone made him out to be," said Cord. "They said he was the next

Abe Lincoln, a sure bet for president, the man this country needed. What they don't say is how Billy Fallows earned a living. He wasn't happy with a senator's income; he decided to hike his pay with drug smuggling, piracy, and white slavery. Poor Eric found out about it, so Fallows ordered him killed." Cord's jaw tightened, remembering.

"I was there in that dockside alley when they ambushed him, and dragged him off to be killed. They sliced me up and left me to die. I went crazy after that, McGee. I found out who the killers were and went after them in a stolen boat with a crew of dockside thugs. We caught them and cut them to shreds, and then I went back for Fallows."

McGee smiled grimly. "You always were a bit headstrong, weren't you, Chris?"

"Still am, I guess. I hid in Fallows's bedroom and waited three days for him to show up. Finally, he came in, with the mayor's wife in his arms. I confronted the bastard, and he admitted everything, and I lost all control and harpooned him and got the hell out of there before half of San Francisco showed up to lynch me."

"And that's when you gave yourself a shave, and started callin' yourself Diamondback?"

Cord nodded.

McGee's red brows furrowed suspiciously. "How do I know you're tellin' the truth? How do I know you didn't just make up all this stuff?"

"You don't." Cord yawned, and stretched out on the bed. "Do you mind if I get a little sleep while you're making up your mind?"

"Jesus," said McGee, shaking his head. "You're a confident son-of-a-bitch, ain't you?"

"Nope. I'm just too tired to care." Cord closed his

eyes and barely heard the sound of the door closing behind the departing captain. The sleep was swift in coming. But it was a troubled slumber, a maddening jumble of dreams in which he was battered about by the raging sea, lashed with ice-cold fingers. Finally, he managed to climb to safety, only to find that the rope he clung to was a hangman's noose, closing around his neck.

Cord awoke with a start, involuntarily grasping at the soft flesh of his throat. The cabin around him was cool and dark, and silent except for the muffled ship sounds. As Cord's dream began to fade, and the knowledge of where he was came back to him, he lay back in the rumpled bedclothes and tried to relax. He was well on his way to San Francisco; McGee would almost certainly keep his secret; and in a few hours, he'd see Victoria Meyers and ask about her urgent summons.

Cord began to relax again, and he was on the brink of falling back to sleep when he realized he was not alone.

"About time you woke up," said Kimberly Bryce. "Move over a bit, would you? You're crushing me."

# 4

Cord groaned and closed his eyes. "If you've come for excitement, I'm afraid you've got the wrong place."

"Don't sell yourself short, cowboy," Kimberly chuckled, bouncing into bed beside him. "All you need is a little incentive."

"More than a little. I almost drowned out there, Kimberly, not to mention suffering near fatal exposure."

"Exposure? I'll show you exposure." Kimberly pressed up against him, and Cord realized that her fancy dress and undergarments were gone. "You know what the best treatment is?"

"Yeah. Sleep." Cord closed his eyes and tried to ignore her, but Kimberly wrapped her arms around him and pressed the full length of her body against his. Cord could feel her breasts, soft and firm against his side, and the tickling mound of her pubic hair against his abdomen. In spite of himself, he was becoming aroused.

"You can sleep all you want, Cord," Kimberly assured him, "as soon as we've finished your *other* treatment." She licked at the base of his throat.

"What if the captain comes back?" asked Cord.

"He won't. They're giving you peace and quiet while you recover."

"Decent of them."

Kimberly traced his jawline with her fingertip. "I need to recover, too, Cord."

"You look fine to me."

"I don't *feel* fine. We could have been killed out there. It's . . . not easy, coming to grips with that." Her fingers touched his lips. "It helps to get close with someone, Cord; it makes things easier to deal with. I don't know why, but it does."

"So I'll be doing you a favor here?"

"That's right." Kimberly ran her fingers through his chest hair. "If it's not too much trouble."

Cord yawned, thinking of the sleep he was missing. Undaunted, Kimberly tickled the hair on his stomach, moving her fingers steadily lower. She traced the path all around his penis, coming tantalizing close but never quite touching it. Despite his exhaustion, Cord could feel himself responding to her sexual teasing.

"Sure you want to sleep?" asked Kimberly. "There are lots of . . . other possibilities."

She tickled under his balls with her forefinger, and Cord involuntarily arched his back. Still tickling, she reached over with her other hand and took a firm hold of his penis. Pleasure swept through Cord's body and she tightened her grip, released it, and tightened it again.

"I hope you don't think I'm too forward," said Cord dryly. The last word was cut short as Kimberly squeezed him again, sending a flare-up of desire throughout his body. She shifted her grip, getting a better hold on him, and bent down to run her tongue stem to stern over his throbbing genitals.

Cord tried to sit up, but Kimberly hooked her legs

across his neck and chest and forced him down again. The show girl shifted her position on Cord's chest until he was pinned to the mattress, his head locked firmly between her legs. Cord made a halfhearted effort to throw her off, but his strength was depleted and he didn't really want her off, anyway.

With Cord held securely under her, Kimberly went for his penis in earnest, drenching it with her tongue, swallowing it whole into the warmth of her throat, caressing his balls with his penis trapped inside her. Then she withdrew, tantalizingly, purposely not touching him until the erection subsided, only to seize him again, with redoubled passion until Cord swelled larger than ever.

Cord raised his head and probed her with his tongue, savoring the flavor like the juice of a finely seasoned sirloin. He took her hips in both arms and pulled her even closer to his tongue's exploring wetness. Kimberly moaned and sucked on his penis even harder than before, like a child determined to pry every last ounce of flavor from a piece of hard candy.

Cord felt the erotic pleasure begin to build, even as he knew it was building in Kimberly. The show girl tried to release his penis, to pull back and deny him the orgasm yet again, but Cord stopped her. With his free hand he reached out and grabbed her long hair, bunching it in his muscular fist, holding Kimberly's head against him. Then he pumped harder and harder, letting the pressure build to a furious intensity, matching every convulsion with a tongue thrust into Kimberly's shivering vagina.

Finally, the explosion came, a volcanic release that emptied all of Cord's milky semen into the show girl's throat. Kimberly convulsed in a spasm of pleasure as Cord arched repeatedly, draining his juices, holding tight to the show girl as he drove her into a devastating climax of her own.

Cord settled back to catch his breath. Kimberly rolled free, panting with exertion, and crawled over to lay by his side. "I thought you were helpless," she said.

"You helped just enough."

"Feeling better?"

"Much, thank you." Cord smiled.

Kimberly snuggled against him, sliding an arm behind his back. Suddenly, she pursed her lips. "Gosh, Cord, your back is hurt bad. Maybe you should get McGee to look at it."

Cord slid away from her. "Nothing to worry about. I got a little scorched running around the *Princess*. I'm sure it'll be fine."

"I hope so." Kimberly rested her head on his chest, looking up at him. "Why are you going to San Francisco, Cord?"

Cord shrugged. "Change of scenery. How about you?"

"I like men," she said simply.

"Yeah, I sort of noticed that. But why San Francisco?"

"Because that's where the men are. I hear they're packed in the streets out here, with no women for miles. So I figure, a theater girl like me, with—let's say—better-than-average looks and a dash of frontier spirit ought to do real well, what with all those red-blooded stallions running around looking to be entertained."

"Makes sense," said Cord. "During the Gold Rush, and the Silver Rush after it, the town was almost all male. Probably because all the young men dropped everything—including their girl friends—and raced out west to get rich. There's still lots more men than women. With all those fellas around, there ought to be a husband for you somewhere.''

Kimberly frowned. "Who wants to get married? I just want men, lots of them, all I can handle." She looked at him earnestly. "How am I doing so far?"

"No complaints here," said Cord.

Kimberly made a contented sound, nestling against his shoulder. Cord closed his eyes and gradually fell asleep. He was still sleeping when the *Aegean* entered San Francisco Bay and put into the Pacific Street Wharf, hours later.

But he woke up fast when loud voices echoed overhead, and a fusillade of rifle shots erupted from the wharf. Something thudded into the side of the boat, and a crewmen yelled, "Load that damned cannon before we're sunk!"

# 5

Cord pulled his shirt from a chair and shrugged into it, before Kimberly could notice his scars. Then he yanked on his pants, boots, and gun belt and was halfway out the door when the show girl roused herself enough to ask, "What's going on?"

"I'll let you know," said Cord.

Diamondback sprinted to the railing of the three-masted clipper, where McGee and a cluster of his men were yelling hoarsely over the side. A burly gang of dockyard workers yelled back at them, brandishing Winchester rifles. Some fired, but they were shooting into the air—for the moment.

"What's the problem?" asked Cord, shouldering his way next to the red-haired captain.

"It's that slime-eating wharf pig, Murchison," snarled McGee, his features ruddy with rage. "He wants to buy some of our cargo, and won't let us unload until he does. Trouble is he wants to buy it at *his* price, not mine."

"What's he trying to buy?"

"Pepper. We've got almost a ton of it in the cargo hold. Murchison has some sort of deal with the local grocers, where he supplies them at a fixed price—but it's three times what he pays us! I figure we can do a hell of a lot better on our own."

"But Murchison controls the docks," Cord surmised, "and he doesn't plan to give you that chance."

"Well, I'm takin' it anyhow." McGee ducked low as another rifle fired, and a bullet whined off the hull. "You fellas want a fight, we'll give you one."

Cord grabbed the captain's hand as he went for the six-shooter at his hip. "You're not going to solve it that way, McGee. I've got another idea. Where's Murchison?"

"On his way over here. He sent a snot-nose bookkeeper up to tell me what I had to sell for, and I sent him right back with a message for Murchison to come over and show himself, in person."

Cord frowned. "What's everyone so mad about?"

"My own fault," McGee admitted. "Guess I got a little too enthusiastic, throwing that bookkeeper fella off the boat." The captain pointed to a spot on the wharf where a crate lay crushed and broken. It looked as if someone had fallen onto it from a great height.

"Always the diplomat," said Cord.

"We'll see." McGee pointed toward a commotion up the street. "That looks like Bob Murchison coming now."

Cord squinted into the sunlight. The disgruntled crowd of laborers parted to reveal an elegant horse-drawn carriage, pulling smoothly onto the docks, led by a team of finely groomed Clydesdales. The carriage door opened and a tall man in a hound's-tooth greatcoat stepped out.

Robert Murchison straightened his collar and cast a disdainful glance at the *Aegean*. He had sharp, birdlike features, with a smallish mouth and a slender, pointed nose. As he stepped forward the men cleared a space for him, like palace guards before royalty.

Murchison stopped at the foot of the *Aegean*'s gangplank and called up, "What's the trouble here, Captain?"

"No trouble," said McGee, barreling down the gangplank. "We're just waiting for you to let us unload our cargo."

Murchison raised an eyebrow as McGee lumbered onto the dock and stopped in front of him, only inches away. Cord and some crewmen were close behind. McGee stabbed a thick finger into Murchison's chest and said, "How about it, snot bucket? Do we unload this stuff around you, or through you?"

Murchison smiled pleasantly. "I'll be happy to unload everything," he explained, "as soon as we've completed our transaction. I understand you were dissatisfied with the terms offered by young Jacobs earlier this morning?"

"You mangy sheepdog . . ." McGee almost lunged for Murchison on the spot, but Cord stopped him with an upraised hand. One of the men in Murchison's party slid a Colt .45 from its holster and held it, pointing at the ground. Several of McGee's men did likewise.

"No deal," said the red-haired captain. "We'll unload it ourselves. Just tell your men to stay out of our way."

"I'm afraid I can't," said Murchison apologetically. "We've got a policy to uphold here, Captain. If we were to allow even a single exception, why, our system of commerce would be irreparably compromised. Surely you understand."

"I understand that you're buying pepper for a hundred bucks and selling it for three times that!"

"Its resale value is not your affair, Captain. Please be careful not to overstep your boundaries."

Diamondback cleared his throat. "Perhaps I can offer a solution."

Murchison eyed him coolly. "You are?"

"Cord Diamondback, free-lance judge. I make a living settling disputes, Mr. Murchison. Some are a lot like this one."

Robert Murchison started to turn away, but hesitated. Something in Cord's calm, colorless eyes interested the dockside merchant, and the name was disturbingly familiar. "Cord Diamondback," he said thoughtfully. "I've heard of you. Not long ago—in Denver, wasn't it?"

He snapped his fingers. "Jay Mellard, the railroad millionaire! *He* hired you. Some sort of railroad problem, and Mellard hired you to settle it, and you did. A pleasure, sir." Murchison held out his hand, not bothering to remove the glove.

Cord shook it anyway. "Maybe I can settle this one, too, sir."

"I'm afraid not," said Murchison, shaking his head. "Dockyard policy is not subject to negotiation. Besides, you're a friend of Beefeater McGee. What assurance would I have of a fair decision?"

"My word," said Cord.

Murchison raised an eyebrow. Cord Diamondback *was* known, even here in San Francisco, for his tough, unrelenting fairness. A man didn't come by that sort of reputation easily. Murchison glanced around at McGee's crewmen, armed and itching for a fight, and his dockyard workers, more than willing to give them one. He didn't mind settling it with violence—once he was out of firing range—but shootouts cost time and money, and were generally bad business. Diplomatic solutions were cheaper.

Murchison looked sharply at McGee. "Will you abide by this man's decision?"

"I surely will." The captain's head bobbed up and down. "Chris—uh . . . Mr. Diamondback here is the straightest man I ever knew."

"Fine. It's a bargain." Murchison faced Cord and said stiffly, "Now tell us, Judge, just how much *should* Captain McGee be paid for his precious pepper stores?"

"One hundred dollars," said Cord promptly.

McGee's face purpled. "You lyin' jackanape! You were supposed to side with *me*, not him!"

"I haven't sided with anyone," said Cord. "I picked the fairest price. There is a condition, though." He looked squarely at Murchison. "You have to buy all the pepper in McGee's stores."

"I don't *need* all of it," said Murchison irritably.

"What you need is irrelevant. Captain McGee has taken a great deal of trouble to bring you two thousand pounds of pepper—and since we've now established a fair price for it, it's only fitting that you purchase the entire supply."

Murchison shrugged. "Fair enough, Cord. I can spare a couple of dollars for a conclusive decision. Especially"—he looked meaningfully at McGee—"considering the resale value."

The captain stood very still, boiling with anger.

Murchison turned to the foremost of his workers and issued rapid orders. "Greeves, have the pepper unloaded and distributed at once. Then assist Captain McGee with the disposition of his remaining cargo. Finally, draw up a purchase order for the *Aegean*'s pepper stores at the agreed-upon price, and pay him from petty cash. Good day, gentlemen."

Robert Murchison spun on his heel and walked briskly back to his carriage. A liveried attendant opened the door for him.

Murchison got in and signaled the driver with a jaunty wave of his hand. In moments the carriage was bolting pell-mell up Pacific Street, heading for the heart of town.

"It better be good," said McGee, turning to face Cord. "What's the goddamned idea, giving it to him at that price?"

"Good business practice," Cord said calmly. "Meeting his price on this one item lets you sell the rest of your stock at your own rate, with no trouble unloading it. If we'd had a gunfight, nobody would win—not you, or Murchison, or even the grocers who receive your goods. Violent solutions profit nobody, McGee. This was the only way."

"But look at the money he'll make resellin' that pepper!"

Cord smiled. "Well, I don't know about that. One of the passengers on the *Brandywine Princess* was an investor, on his way to meet a spice fleet from Singapore. Word has it they've got tons of pepper, more than they can possibly sell—so much that they'll probably take most of it and dump it into the bay for landfill." Cord leaned against the starboard rail. "How do you suppose that'll affect the market?"

McGee grinned slyly. "It'll drive the price down, won't it?"

"That's right. The fleet's due at any minute. As soon as they hit town, the bottom will drop out of the market and the stuff won't be worth a dime a barrel. Good thing you managed to sell your whole stock before they got here."

McGee burst out laughing, a deep rumbling guffaw that sounded vaguely like an earthquake. He slapped Cord on the back, almost toppling him. "You ain't such a bad judge after all, huh, Cord?"

"Just doing my job." Cord headed for the cabin to round up his things.

"But *why* can't I come with you?" asked Kimberly Bryce, tugging at Cord's shirtsleeve. They were standing on the dock, beside the steadily growing pile of cargo unloaded from the *Aegean*'s hold.

"I told you, I've got business in town," said Cord. "Personal business."

"With another girl?"

"Yes. She's an old friend, someone I haven't seen in a long time. She's expecting me."

Kimberly nodded stiffly. "I guess this is good-bye, then."

"Don't take it so hard," said Cord. "I know I'm irreplaceable—but you *do* have all these red-blooded stallions to pick from." Cord waved his arm, taking in the grand sweep of dockyard workers and seaside businessmen covering the wharf. "Only takes one, you know."

"Are you kidding? I want *all* of them—one at a time."

Kimberly gave him a parting kiss, then strolled off toward a brawny young dockwalloper, hefting a crate. "I'm new in town," she said shyly. "Can you tell me a good place to stay . . . ?"

Cord grinned and tightened the saddle on the horse he'd purchased at a nearby stable, a strong, auburn mustang. He loaded his gear into the saddlebags and put his rifle in the scabbard. Then he mounted up and set off for Victoria Meyers's Telegraph Hill address.

All around him was the bustling activity that filled each morning in San Francisco. Merchants haggled under the shade of a striped awning; brokers scurried from shop to shop, seeking the best price for a boatload of goods. At the corner stood a fish market, with the finer specimens of the morning's catch displayed proudly in the store's front window.

The dockside air was filled with the smell of freshly unloaded shrimp and lobster, a smell that Cord savored like an old friend's handshake. More than any other, San Francisco was *his* city; he felt an odd sense of communion with the rough-and-tumble bayside community, a feeling of belonging that was hard to put into words.

The city's history was astounding. During those first, frantic Gold Rush days, when wealth-seekers poured in from all over America, the port of Yerba Buena Cove had grown faster than any city on earth: from a collection of sodden dockside huts in 1848 to a sprawling, full-fledged metropolis barely five years later.

Not that the progress had been a smooth transition period. In its short history, San Francisco had been ravaged by fire half a dozen times, often the work of vandals and arsonists seeking protection money from frightened shopkeepers. And the unsanitary conditions of the city's poorer sections made them ripe for the spreading of contagious diseases.

But nothing had stopped the mad growth of young San Francisco. Scores of developers had rebuilt the devastated city, and rebuilt it again after each new disaster. The city's official seal was a phoenix, rising from the ashes—the symbol of rebirth and renewal, in the face of fiery holocaust.

In a way, the phoenix was Cord's symbol, too. Cord had achieved his own rebirth after the brutal baptism that had left Billy Fallows a bloody corpse and made Christopher Deacon a wanted man. Hunted and hated, he'd taken the Indian name of Diamondback and started his life all over again.

The problem was to preserve his new identity.

Cord was uncomfortably aware of the number of acquaintances he'd made in San Francisco; any one of them could expose his secret and end his new career forever. But he was older now, his hair was cut differently, and he'd shaved off the thick brown beard always worn by Christopher Deacon. Besides, he had the advantage of surprise—no one would expect a criminal as notorious as Deacon to go anywhere near the scene of his crime.

The road was steeper now, as Cord urged his horse up Montgomery Street toward Telegraph Hill. Over Cord's shoulder was a breathtaking view of the Golden Gate, and the schooners and steamers plying its waters. Before him was an avenue of graceful houses and mansions, many in the elegant Victorian style, with arches, balusters, and impressive bay windows.

At the corner was Victoria Meyers's home, a cleanly built Tudor mansion easily dwarfed by its extravagant neighbors. The mansion was paneled in redwood and painted in earth-tone shades of brown and gray. Double-hung windows overlooked a wide, arched doorway. In front of the door were two men in jeans, jackets, and Lone Star boots, wearing Sheriff's Model Peacemaker .45's at the hip.

The man on the left, a thick-bodied cowboy with oily skin, tapped his partner and pointed straight at Cord. "That's him, Hank," he said with obvious excitement. "Damnfool showed here after all, just like they said."

Hank was thick-bodied, too, but with a much cleaner complexion. "Durned if you ain't right, Pete," he said, gripping the butt of his Peacemaker. "Let's get him."

# 6

---

Cord dismounted and looped the reins around a lightpost. "You boys looking for someone?"

Hank came up to Cord and faced him eye to eye, still fingering his gun butt. "Not anymore, we ain't. You the fella comin' to visit Miss Victoria?"

"That's me," said Cord. "You boys her chaperone or something?"

Pete frowned, rubbing his chin. Suddenly he laughed. "Oh, I get it! Like we was guardin' her against some fella comin' along and makin' her pregnant, or somethin'. Hey, that's a good one."

"Shut up, Pete," said Hank, keeping his eyes on Diamondback. "Listen, mister, I'll say this just once. You're comin' with us right now, and that's a fact. Now, you comin' quiet, or not?"

"Depends on where we're going," said Cord.

"No, it don't. Because you're comin' either way—and you can do it easy or hard. Ain't that right, Pete?"

Pete chuckled to himself. "Chaperones. That's a good one."

"Dammit, Pete—"

"I'm listenin', I'm listenin'!" Pete snapped to attention. "What am I supposed to be doin'?"

"You're supposed to be helpin', is all. Do you think

you could hush up long enough to earn that five dollars Mr. Mars gave us?"

"Okay," said Pete petulantly. "You don't have to get all riled up about it."

Hank shook his head disgustedly and turned back to Cord. Cord smiled and pressed the barrel of his Schofield .45 into Hank's breastbone. "Think I'll go in and see the lady now," he said.

Hank stepped back, hands pawing the air. Pete stepped back, too. Cord started past them, courteously touching his hat brim.

Pete dove for Cord's gun.

Cord sidestepped the move and leveled his gun at Pete's chest. Pete turned around and charged again. Cord could easily have gunned him down, but he didn't want to—and his hesitation was all it took for Pete to smash into his midsection and knock him to the ground.

Pete grabbed Cord's neck and tried to throttle him, his fingers clamping hard on Cord's windpipe. Cord picked a spot behind Pete's ear and clubbed him with the butt of the Schofield. Pete went slack but Cord kept under him for cover, banking on the fact that Hank wouldn't risk putting a slug into Pete's body.

He was wrong.

Hank fired anyway; a bullet hit the gravel by Cord's ear, and two more thumped into Pete's back. Pete's body jerked like a calf under a branding iron. Cord fired from Pete's armpit, unable to aim properly but hoping to spook his opponent. Hank ducked back, scrambling for cover.

Cord was trying for a better shot when Victoria Meyers said, "That's enough."

He looked at her and caught his breath.

Victoria stood in the doorway of her home, covering Hank with an American Arms sawed-off shotgun. It looked very comfortable in her hands. She was a slender, smallish woman, modestly dressed, with a chignon of dark brown hair. She wasn't beautiful, but her looks were cunningly attractive. Cord liked to compare Victoria's appeal to the underlying theme of a symphony—always there, never too obvious, emerging at odd moments when one least expected to find it.

Like right now, Cord thought, rolling Pete off himself and getting to his feet. He couldn't explain Victoria's allure, but its strength was undeniable. He wondered if Hank felt it, too.

"You'd better take that man to the hospital," Victoria said, gesturing with the shotgun barrel. "If he dies, it's murder."

"But I wasn't tryin' to shoot *him*," Hank protested. "I was gunnin' for the other fella. Pete just got in the way, like always."

Victoria shrugged. "Shame to get hanged for a mistake like that." She raised her weapon. "Or shot."

"I'm goin'," said Hank hastily, bending over to lift Pete's body. He hoisted the wounded man onto his shoulders and set off down the hill. Cord heard him muttering, "Still say it ain't murder 'less you shoot the right guy . . ."

"Nice to see you, Vicky," said Cord.

Victoria set down the shotgun, leaning it inside the doorway. "It's been a while, hasn't it?" She studied him, raising a critical eyebrow. "I don't like you without the beard, Cord. You look a little less . . . masculine."

Cord crossed the distance between them in four long strides. "Appearances can be deceiving."

Victoria watched him, not speaking. Cord smiled. With a sigh she leaned into him, smoothing the fabric of his shirt with her fingertips, savoring the feel and smell of this man she loved but so seldom touched. Cord brushed her hair with the rough skin of his palm, pulling loose Victoria's barrettes to let the dark locks tumble over her shoulders.

"We'd better go inside," he suggested, "before we start violating the blue laws."

She nodded, leading him in. Once indoors, Victoria carefully locked the front door and fastened the chain, in the oddly fastidious way Cord always found appealing. Cord had once told her that if anyone broke in while they were making love he'd be more than willing to pay the damages. She'd chuckled and said she wasn't locking them out, she was locking him *in*.

"I've missed you," said Cord.

"You, too," said Victoria. "And I think about you much more than a woman should. Every time some red-nosed farmer comes in here and says he's got to find that Diamondback fella, well, I envy him—because he gets to track you down in some two-horse town while I'm stuck here writing wills and signing bankruptcy forms." She smiled wryly. "Half the people go after you; I can't *imagine* what you end up doing for them."

"Improvising, mostly," Cord admitted. "You'd be surprised how many folks are only looking for a pat on the head and a cherry soda. But once in a while a tough one comes along, and that keeps it interesting."

"I've got a tough one," said Victoria. "I'm not even sure you can help, but I had to try. It's about Deborah."

Cord's smile vanished. "What's happened? Where is she?"

"I don't know. That's the problem." Victoria held him tightly, and in her outwardly calm voice was a note of real fear. Cord knew how Victoria loved her daughter; if Deborah was in trouble, Victoria would do anything to help her. Cord had never met Deborah—she'd been only ten at the time of Fallows's murder—but he was just as determined to help.

Victoria squeezed his hand. "Let me fix you some coffee, Cord, and we'll talk about it."

She led him into a tastefully furnished kitchen, where she served coffee in little cups of hand-painted porcelain. Cord gulped the fresh-brewed coffee by the cupful, but the lady's cup was untouched.

"Tell me about Deborah," said Diamondback.

Victoria sighed. "She started seeing a fella, Cord— yes, she's old enough now—and she started getting serious about him. Fergus Rheingold, a sailor—she met him in a dockside bar. Nice boy, although I really thought she could do better.

"Well, one day he went off to Cape Horn on a ship called the *Orpheus*, and Deborah didn't hear from him for six months. She kept waiting, counting the days till he was due to return. Finally, the day arrived, but his ship didn't—not then, or the next day, or the next.

"Just as Deborah was giving up, she got a message that Rheingold had come in, after all—and desperately needed to see her. I never saw the messenger before, or since. She left with him and never came back."

"It's an odd one," Cord conceded. "Did you report it?"

"Of course! I went all the way to the city council. I talked to a councilman named Heywood Mars, a smooth-talking scoundrel I liked not at all, and said if they couldn't help I'd damned well bring in someone who could. That's when the sideshow boys showed up outside to discourage visitors."

"I'm surprised you let them stay around," said Cord.

She smiled. "I wanted them to meet you, face to face. But that's off the subject. Will you help? I know it's dangerous for you to be here, but you're the best chance I have."

Cord set down his coffee cup. "I'll try. Maybe a few questions around the waterfront can turn up something. Meantime, I'll stay alert and try not to stand too close to any 'Christopher Deacon Wanted' posters."

"It's no joke, Cord," said Victoria earnestly. "You could die from this, you know. Be careful."

"I will." Cord drained his cup and stood up. "Well, I'd better get started."

"Not yet." She stopped him, with a hand on his shoulder. "First . . . I need to love you, Cord. It's been so long. I need to love you, right now."

Cord nodded solemnly, catching the worry in Victoria's voice, the need for intimacy in the face of gathering fear. She stood quite close to him and whispered, "Now."

Cord took the string closure on her blouse between the thumb and forefinger and tugged at it, undoing the delicate knot. With one finger he separated the collar, exposing the milky skin of her throat. Then he widened the opening, deftly loosening the buttons of Victoria's blouse until he came to the edge of a satin camisole.

"It's brand-new," she explained. "I bought it from a mail-order catalog for a special occasion. You're the first man to see it, Cord."

"Worth waiting for," he said.

Cord finished opening her blouse and spread it wide to examine the camisole. It was frilled satin, a rich, dark red, like wine from a forgotten cellar. Victoria's modest breasts poked over the top of it, small but perfectly formed. Cord touched her nipples and felt them respond, coming instantly erect under his calloused fingers.

"I *have* missed you," said Victoria.

"Me, too," said Cord, with feeling. The hardest part of his fugitive life-style was losing Vicky, being unable to see her more than once or twice a year. But that made these visits all the more delicious. Cord gave her breasts a parting caress and moved to open her belt, finding a double row of buttons at the waist of her skirt.

"I wish you'd wear simpler clothing," he said, shaking his head. "Romancing you is like climbing Mount McKinley. By the time a fella gets up there, he just might forget why he set out in the first place."

"If it slips your mind," Victoria assured him, "I'll refresh your memory."

Cord undid the last of the buttons and slid Victoria's skirt and petticoats over her smooth legs. They were shapely but quite pale, since the brown-haired lawyer was too modest to be seen out of doors in anything but a full skirt. Cord pondered the paradox of Vicky's morals that kept her from exposing even her ankles outside, although she liked to be fully naked before she entered the bedroom for lovemaking.

Cord slid the camisole over her lean figure and dropped it around her ankles. Victoria moved to undress him, in turn, but before she could, he took her in a tender embrace and kissed her again and again.

"You're not making it easier," she said breathlessly, wriggling free.

Victoria started with his boots and worked upward. She undid his jeans and worked them down over Cord's muscular legs, brushing his penis with a deft, almost accidental stroke of her forefinger. Cord felt himself responding to her touch in a way that was enriched and multiplied by the abiding love he felt for her.

Then she unbuttoned his shirt and slid it off. Victoria stepped behind him and caressed the scarred skin of his back, stroking the jagged surface with a touch that spoke of cool, healing waters from a mountain-fed stream. For Cord the caress was unbearably sensual. His scars were a burden he kept totally secret, a part of himself he could never share with even the most intimate of lovers.

But Victoria knew his past—and loved him all the more for it. To her the scars were proof of Cord's character, like the ritual cuts inflicted on African tribesmen at the onset of maturity. Cord had once told her how he viewed the phoenix as a symbol of his own life, and she thought the metaphor was a good one.

"You remember where the bedroom is, Cord?"

Cord nodded. Wordlessly, he led her up a carpeted stairway to a richly furnished bedroom, with a queen-sized canopy bed sporting satin sheets and embroidered pillowcases. Sunlight streamed through a high corner window. Victoria pulled back the sheets and invited Cord to get in first. He rolled under the covers and Victoria slid in beside him.

They kissed.

It took a long time. Cord put his arms around her and the two of them rolled over and over across the bed, unwilling to break it off. Soon the sheets were tangled and Cord found himself securely wrapped against Victoria's body, enshrouded in the feather-soft satin.

Cord closed his eyes, luxuriating in Victoria's closeness, trying to focus his attention on every square inch of her skin against his. Victoria's hands kneaded his back, caressing the cruelly scarred flesh, sending an erotic thrill through Cord with each lingering finger touch.

Cord's back arched as he rolled on top of Victoria, binding the sheets even tighter, her smell filling his nostrils as she locked her arms behind his back and clung to him fiercely. Cord tightened his own embrace as he felt himself entering her. All his love for Victoria, all the passion of their separation of years, suddenly burst through its fragile seams and exploded in a sunburst of pleasure, like a prizefighter throwing a knockout punch or a marksman scoring a bull's-eye.

Victoria screamed as Cord filled her to bursting with his devastating erection. As Cord sprayed his seed into her, pulling her close with the full power of his thickly muscled forearms, Victoria felt an ecstatic tide wash over her, an oceanic orgasm that shunted aside all other feelings. She knew only that she was the love partner of Cord Diamondback, and he was claiming her, and the joy of surrender to him was the purest delight she would ever know.

For several long, languid moments they just lay there, pressed together between the smooth, silken sheets. Victoria hummed to herself, a tune Cord couldn't identify. Finally, she held up her hand and said, "Tell me one thing, Cord."

"What's that?"

"It's probably none of my business—"

"Never stopped you before."

"—but I was wondering . . ." She looked at him with obvious curiosity, and finally blurted out her question. "What did you ever do with that mail-order bride someone sent you six months ago?"

Cord laughed aloud. "Miss Penelope? I ought to

throttle you for forwarding *that* particular problem. Didn't you tell her I wasn't looking for a family?"

"Not my job," said Victoria. "I figured it would dawn on her sooner or later. But of all the ranchers, miners, cardsharps, and horse thieves who've tramped through my office looking for Cord Diamondback, she's the one I've wondered about the most."

"Don't worry," said Cord. "I found her a nice young lad—or rather, *she* found *him*—and the two of them settled down in a town you never heard of to raise a flock of offspring. They're probably still out there."

"And you never laid a hand on her in the meantime?"

"Well—hardly ever." Diamondback rolled on top of her suddenly and looked straight into her eyes. "When did you become so jealous?"

Victoria flushed, suddenly conscious of the full length of his body against hers. "I was just curious, that's all. And it seemed so unfair that she could go to you while I . . . well, it just seemed unfair."

Cord kissed her, taking his time. "I'm here now," he said. "Let's enjoy it while we can."

After a while, they slept. Victoria came awake suddenly with the feeling that their slumber had been so deep, so all-consuming, that endless hours must have passed. But the sunlight slanting through the high window was only a little farther down, so the morning must still be early.

Victoria nestled into Cord's arms again, waiting for him to awaken. She wasn't going to hurry him. Victoria liked lying in Cord's arms, her cherished dream all the years he'd been away—and she was not eager to end it, even for a while.

But a grimmer reason was the terrible danger he'd be facing, quite soon. Cord was returning to the Barbary Coast, where his secret would face its greatest test. He was *known* there, as Christopher Deacon, and the risk of exposure was terrifying. The first time an old brawling chum spotted him and raised a commotion, Cord would be clapped in irons and strung up from a lightpost—if he was lucky.

Victoria held him tightly. Never before had Cord Diamondback's violent past been so close to catching up with him. And if it did, she could only blame herself. In the cool, still light of morning Victoria Meyers wondered if the risk to Cord was worth the small chance of finding her daughter alive.

But her choice had already been made—and only Cord Diamondback could decide the outcome.

# 7

"Fergus Rheingold? Sure, I heard of 'im. Ornery little cuss."

The old sailor tamped a wad of tobacco into a hand-carved pipe and leaned back in his chair. Loud voices came from the next table, and someone pounded the keys on an out-of-tune piano. "Who wants to know about him?"

"A friend," said Cord.

"How good a friend?"

Cord stuffed a five-dollar bill into the old man's shirt pocket. The old man pulled it out and inspected the denomination, under the flickering glare of a barroom lantern. Satisfied, he replaced it and waited for Cord's next question.

"When did you last see him?" asked Cord.

"Not long ago," said the old man. "Listen, not much gets by without old Blind Tom hearin' of it."

"Good for you," said Cord. "Where was he?"

Blind Tom gave him a ferocious look. "Aren't you goin' to ask me about my name?"

"What about it?"

"Lot of folks think it's strange to call me Blind Tom when I can see as good as they can." Blind Tom struck a match on the seat of his trousers and lit his pipe with it. "Want to know how I got the name?"

"Tell me later."

"I was lookout for this cargo ship," said Blind Tom doggedly. "Middle of the night, fog so thick you could chop it up and have it for dinner. Well, I'm up there in the crow's nest, see, real tired on account of my insomnia, and suddenly I spot this mermaid out splashin' around, a real live mermaid, with scales and flippers and the biggest damned set of tits you ever saw."

Blind Tom shrugged. "Naturally, I don't want to disturb her, so I just sit there and watch her, real quiet-like. I was still watchin' her when the ship hit a reef, and that's when I woke up." He winced. "Worst wreck you ever saw, four survivors including me, and every one of 'em said I musta been stone blind to let us get that close. Blind Tom, they called me. What you drinkin', mister?"

Cord finished his Scotch, then signaled for two more. When they came he thrust one in Tom's direction. "You were telling me about Rheingold."

"Oh, yeah, good ol' Fergus. Real hell-raiser, he was, maybe still is if you're after him. What'd he do this time?"

"Nothing," Cord assured him. "I owe him some money, but I have to find him fast because I'm shipping out in the morning. I'd be grateful if you could help me."

"Can't," said Tom. "I don't keep in touch with him much. But I'll tell you who does." He leaned in close, practically whispering in Cord's ear. "You know the Cock's Comb, over on Jackson Street?"

"I've heard of it."

"Good. Go over there and ask for Smitty Welch.

Tell 'im Tom sent you and I said it's all right. If you ask 'im nice, you shouldn't have any trouble.''

"Thanks.'' Cord stood up to leave, tossing a bill on the grimy tabletop. Blind Tom nodded and sipped at his Scotch. Cord turned suddenly and caught the eye of the man who'd been following him for the past thirty minutes, standing by the bar. The man averted his eyes.

Cord studied him. He was tall and thin, with a scruffy widow's peak atop a sloping forehead. He was nursing a glass of something that might have been vermouth. Cord started past him and noticed a quick, barely perceptible signal to a person or persons behind him.

Cord stepped outside, showing no concern, then sprinted for the nearest alley. He reached it just as Widow's Peak burst out the door, with two brawny hoodlums behind him. One of them pointed right at Cord, and all three started forward. Cord ran the length of the alley and found it led nowhere, into a three-sided dead end where Widow's Peak and his friends would have an irresistible target.

In one corner of the alley was a packing crate, still reeking of fish oil and food smells. Cord tried to duck behind it, but it was much too flimsy to use as cover against bullets. He wondered what else to try.

"Don't worry, he's stuck in there,'' said a voice from the street. "All we gotta do is smoke him out.''

"You sure it's him?'' asked someone else. "I mean, what would the son-of-a-bitch be doing here?''

"I don't know, and I don't care. But that reward's more money than I ever seen in one place, and I aim to get a piece of it.''

Cord knew the voice: it was one of the pirates he'd hired to track down Eric's killers years ago. At the time he'd been so eager to snare the culprits that he'd hired anyone, no questions asked—and all of them had gotten to know Christopher Deacon. Now someone had spotted him, and planned to profit from it.

Cord drew his Schofield. A little jog in the alley hid him from the view of his pursuers, but it wouldn't be long before they started in—and there weren't many places he could go. His best hope was an ambush. Cord pressed against the side of a building, partly concealed by the packing crate.

"Still say you should have told Marty about this," said the second voice. "Just to be on the safe side."

"And split the money four ways? Christ, Bobby, you're dumb sometimes. I don't even know why we brought you in. Hush now, maybe he's layin' for us."

The voices broke off, but the soft footsteps kept coming. Cord looked around. Across the alley was a narrow window, too high and too small to climb, but perfect for a distraction. He picked up a rock and tossed it at the window, shattering it.

"Shit, he's gettin' away!" Bobby yelled.

All three bolted pell-mell down the alley, guns drawn. Cord waited for them to come abreast of him and stood up from concealment, firing. Widow's Peak went down with his skull ripped open, the right side of his body twitching. The middle gunman took slugs in the shoulder and stomach. He whirled around, clawing at himself, like a frenzied ballerina. The third man shot back at Cord, coming so close the near misses sprayed brick splinters in his hair.

Cort put a hole in the man's solar plexus. Blood gushed out like wine from a cask. The man raised his gun, seemed to change his mind, and lowered it again. Cord finished him with a bullet to the brain.

"Mighty fine shootin', you ask me," said a booming voice from the alley mouth. Cord turned to find Beefeater McGee striding toward him, grinning hugely. "You and these fellas have a dispute over something?"

"Yeah." Cord holstered his gun and started forward. "Let's go. I'll tell you about it on the way."

"Where are we goin'?"

"Tell you that on the way, too."

Beefeater shrugged and followed Cord with a wry glance backward at the decimated gunmen. Widow's Peak had finally stopped twitching; his expression was mildly curious, like a child seeing its first butterfly. The others didn't look like much of anything.

"This is it," said Cord. Before them was a weathered old tavern, even seedier than the last one, with a hanging sign that read COCK'S COMB over a picture of a banty rooster. Shouts came from inside, and the sound of breaking glass.

McGee shook his head. "You really think this'll lead you to that lawyer friend's daughter? Seems pretty unlikely to me."

"One way to find out."

Cord stepped inside, and immediately ducked aside as a broken bottle sailed through the air and shattered against the doorjamb. "Sorry," said an apologetic voice from one of the tables. "Thought you were someone else."

McGee rubbed his palms together. "Want me to kill that fella for ya, Cord?"

"Not yet, McGee," said Cord, raising his hand. "First let's do what we came here for." He wound his way between the tables to a greasy, full-length bar. At the base of the bar was a brass spittoon, often aimed at but rarely hit by the tobacco-chewing patrons. Behind the bar were three long shelves with dirty, uncorked bottles, and a space on the wall where a mirror or picture used to be.

"What'll you have?" asked the bartender. He was tall and wide, impossibly well built, with bushy blond hair and babylike features. There was blood on his bar apron.

"Two whiskeys," said Cord, slapping a bill on the counter, "and I'd like to know which of these folks is Smitty Welch."

"None of 'em. Smitty's upstairs." The bartender filled two glasses from an unlabeled bottle. "Look, if you want to kill 'im, do it quiet, okay? Gunshots upset the patrons down here."

Cord grinned. "I'll remember that." He drained his glass and started for the stairs, with McGee close behind. Cord noticed that the steps creaked badly, a dead giveaway for anyone out to get the drop on old Smitty.

At the head of the stairs were three doors. One was ajar, revealing a filthy bathroom. One was labeled ERNEST FOSDICK, PROPRIETOR. The third was unmarked, but taking place behind it was a shrill argument between a man and a woman. Cord caught the phrase ". . . promised to take care of me . . ."

Cord knocked loudly. "Anybody home?"

Instantly, the argument subsided. The man's voice asked, "Who is it? What do you want?"

"I want to talk to Smitty Welch. There's money in it. Blind Tom sent me."

"Horseshit!" said the man, but the woman's voice said, "Let him in, Smitty. Maybe it's true."

"Yeah, and maybe it's Donatelli's boys come to shoot my face off. Hey, how do I know you folks ain't lyin'?"

McGee put his shoulder into the door and snapped it clean off its hinges. Smitty went for his gun, but Cord was faster. The other man was still groping for the gun belt he'd draped over a chair when Cord leveled his Schofield and said, "Guess you'll have to take our word for it."

Smitty Welch shrugged and dropped the gun belt. He was lying on a four-poster bed, dressed in his underwear, with a not overly attractive redhead beside him. The redhead was burrowing under the bedclothes to protect her modesty. Cord pulled up the chair with Smitty's gun belt on it and sat down.

"Tell me about Fergus Rheingold," he said.

Smitty licked his lips. "You said there was money in it."

Cord pulled a five-dollar bill from his pocket and pressed it into Smitty's palm. Smitty frowned and said, "Make it ten."

"Five's fine. Tell me about Rheingold."

Smitty looked at Cord, and McGee standing beside him, and shrugged. "Not much to tell. He's dead. Been dead for goin' on four days now."

"How'd he die?"

"He got sick, same as the other three. Fergus lived the longest. The others were already dead when they pulled him off the life raft."

"Slow down a minute," said Cord, shaking his head. "They found him on a life raft?"

"That's right. Washed into the bay four days ago, with three dead men and Fergus sick as a puppy dog. Weren't long before old Fergus died, too. No sign of the ship or the other crew, and Fergus weren't in no shape to tell us."

"Okay, one more thing," said Cord. "What was he sick with? They must have done an autopsy."

"A what?"

"They must have found out what killed him. Maybe you heard what it was."

Smitty shrugged. "Maybe I did. Word gets around, you know, if a fella bothers to listen."

Cord waited.

"The plague," said Smitty. "Byoo-bonic plague. Poor bastard never had a chance. You know what I think happened?" Smitty hiked up his shorts and leaned forward. "The whole ship came down with it. Old Fergus and his buddies, they saw it comin' and tried to sneak off on that raft. But by then they had it, too, so they died just like the rest. And that boat, well, it's still out there somewheres, a death ship lookin' for a home." He grinned. "Nice story, huh?"

"It'll do." Cord gave him another five dollars. "That's to get the door fixed. Come on, McGee, we're finished here."

McGee looked crestfallen. "Don't you want me to break this guy's knees or something?"

"What for?"

"Hell, I don't know. Because he's ugly. Who cares?"

Cord ignored him and started downstairs. Reluctantly, McGee followed him. Cord was lost in thought as he crossed the raucous barroom and headed for the door.

Once, during a whaling trip, Cord had seen the effects of bubonic plague firsthand. The epidemic had swept through the Chinese mainland, killing millions, filling whole streets with putrefying bodies where the infection would only breed, and flourish, and infect still more. Whole populations had been annihilated; some villages had been wiped out to the last man.

One scene in particular stayed with him. In one

seaport town where they'd stopped—but not stayed—Cord had seen a dog in the street, gnawing a bone. The dog was a gray-brown mongrel, scruffy and lean, quite a bit like the schnauzer puppy he'd played with as a boy. Beside the dog was a young, quite beautiful Chinese girl in a burgundy silk dress. The girl was lying face up in the middle of the road, looking oddly serene. The bone the dog was gnawing was part of her forearm.

"You worried about the plague, Cord?" asked McGee, clapping him painfully on the shoulder.

"Worried doesn't cover it," said Cord. "You remember the village of Chang Shu?"

"The plague town? Hell, yeah. But that was on the wrong side of the ocean, Cord. You don't think that could happen here?"

Cord said nothing. For the truth was that it *could* happen here, easily. He tried to picture the impact of a plague epidemic in the wet, wintry climate of year-end San Francisco. It would spread like a wild brushfire; sanitation was dismal in the city's poorer sections, and the flea-carrying rats thought to spread the infection were rampant here. The mortalities would be uncountable.

Cord shuddered. If the *Orpheus* was a plague carrier—and the disease got loose in San Francisco—the bayside city would be lucky to survive it.

# 8

"What now?" asked McGee, pouring himself another brandy.

Cord toyed with a shot glass. "We need to find out more about this plague ship," he decided. "Nautical records might turn up something. I might even have a talk with your friend Bob Murchison."

"No friend of mine," McGee snorted. "If it was up to me—"

"*That's him!*" said a strident voice.

Cord turned to find Hank, the gunman from outside Victoria's house, pointing a finger right at him. "That's the guy, all right. He visited that lady lawyer this morning and shot Pete twice in the back."

"Fine," said a broad, muscular man in a bright red shirt. Hank and the red-shirted man were part of a six-man gang, shunned by the bar's other patrons. They marched forward like a precision drill team, to block Cord and McGee from leaving.

"Let's take 'em," said the red-shirted man. "But no guns, 'less they shoot first. The six of us can handle these two."

The gang started forward. Tables and chairs were deserted in their path, as casual drinkers fled the newly drawn battleground. The bartender shrugged his shoulders and absently polished a glass.

"Which ones you want?" asked McGee, studying their opponents.

Cord considered it. "Give me Hank—he's the dumb-looking one with the red hair; also, the guy behind him and the leader of the gang. You can have the rest."

"But I wanted the leader!" said McGee.

Cord shrugged. "You drive a hard bargain." He was about to suggest a substitute when the six men rushed them, shouting hoarsely.

The first man to reach them lost two teeth and consciousness when Cord's right hook hit his jawbone. The next man stumbled over his fallen buddy and fell stomach first onto McGee's ham-hock fist. Before McGee could throw him off, the red-shirted man grabbed him by the throat and held on as two more thugs broke chairs over him.

Cord wanted to help, but he had problems of his own. Despite the leader's instructions, Hank was drawing his Colt from its holster. Cord upended a table and dove under it as Hank fired twice, perforating the pine tabletop. Cord rolled to a stop at Hank's feet, grabbed both ankles, and pulled Hank's legs out from under him. Hank went down, firing uselessly at the ceiling. Cord stepped on his gun hand and yanked the weapon away from him.

Glass broke over Cord's head, and the floor rushed up to meet him. He caught himself on both hands and tried to regain his feet, but a jackbooted kick sent him rolling sideways, clutching his stomach. Hank's Colt clattered to the floor.

Cord's assailant was a short man with arms like dock pilings, smiling cruelly. He drew back for another kick, but Cord threw a chair in his way, rolling clear. The short man cursed and smashed the chair aside. Cord pulled himself upright, gripping the edge of the bar, fighting to regain his balance. Fuzzy points of light swam in and out of his vision as the short man started in again.

Cord went at him with a one-two combination, but his timing was off and the short man countered both punches. Then the man hit Cord hard in the solar plexus and smashed him backward with an uppercut to the throat. Cord hit the wall and saw Hank scrambling across the floor, going for the lost revolver.

The short man snickered and moved in again.

Cord threw a lazy right at him, a punch that missed on purpose. But it set him up for a backward elbow smash into the base of the short man's skull. He grunted and pitched forward, wrapping his arms around Cord's waist. Cord grabbed for his Schofield, but couldn't reach it because of the short man's bear hug.

Hank started shooting.

Cord grabbed the short man's gun, still in its holster. The short man tried to protest, but broke off as one of Hank's slugs caught him between the shoulder blades. Before Hank could try again, Cord emptied the short man's gun into his rib cage. Hank hit the floor and stayed there.

A deafening crash drew Cord's attention. McGee had taken the red-shirted man and driven him head first into the floor, breaking clean through the floorboards. McGee left him that way, and turned to the last gang member still conscious.

"What should I break first, Cord?" asked the captain good-naturedly. "Those elbows are awful temptin', wouldn't you say?"

"I prefer the knees," Cord admitted, "but before you get started, maybe our young friend would like to tell us who sent him here and why."

"Just one elbow, for starters," McGee suggested, "and you can question him while I break the other one."

The intruder turned white. He was a youngish man, blond-haired, with overlarge features that weren't quite centered on his face. "Mr. Mars sent us," he said earnestly, avoiding McGee's eyes. "We were supposed to bring you fellas before the city council for some questions. He gave us all five dollars to do it. Look, here's the money, you can have it."

Hastily, he pulled a crumpled fiver from a pocket of his jeans. Cord took it and said, "Why does the council want to see us?"

"How do I know? Something to do with that Meyers woman. Do you think they're gonna explain it to guys like us?"

"Probably not," Cord mused. "You know, Captain McGee, I'm a little curious about why these people want to see us. I believe I'd like to talk to them."

McGee rubbed his bearded chin. "Guess I would, too, Cord. Do you think this fella could manage to take us over and introduce us?"

The young man swallowed hard. "Uh, glad to," he mumbled.

They hadn't gone far when Cord reined in his horse. "Just a minute," he said. "Isn't City Hall over that way?"

"Well, yeah," said the younger man, slowing his horse. "We're not exactly going to City Hall. You see, this isn't a regular session of the council. It's kind of . . . uh . . . a special meeting."

"Where at?"

He pointed up and forward, at a massive building that dominated the skyline. Cord whistled; they were heading for Market Street's Palace Hotel, the largest hotel in America. A masterpiece of design, it had a seven-story atrium for incoming carriages and over seven thousand bay windows. Cord reflected that the hotel probably had more guests than the whole population of the last town he'd visited.

"Get a load of this place, would you?" said McGee. "Who'd want to spend this much money on a fancy-lookin' flophouse?"

"Ask William Ralston, the millionaire," said Cord. "This hotel was an obsession for him, took him five years and seven million dollars to build. They opened up a special furniture store just to supply the place."

McGee eyed him narrowly. "How come you know so much about it? And don't tell me hotels interest you."

Cord shrugged. "Never know when you might need one."

Soon they came to the base of the structure, a vast square building covering two and a half acres. They left the horses with the hotel's attendants and stepped into the cavernous lobby. Guests bustled about, casting self-important glances at the newcomers as they bustled across the plush-carpeted floor. Doormen sprang to attention when Cord walked over and slammed his palm on the bell.

"Yes, sir," said a clerk, appearing from nowhere.

"Mr. Mars is expecting us," said Cord simply. "Do you have a room key for us?"

The clerk raised an eyebrow. "This is very irregular."

"It's an emergency. Didn't he tell you how important this is?"

"Well, yes . . ."

"Is there some problem?"

The clerk looked around for his superior, but couldn't see him. Finally, he shrugged and reached behind him. "Room 503, middle of the hall," he said feebly.

"Thanks." Cord snatched the key and led McGee and their would-be abductor up five flights of carpeted stairs. The stairway was teeming with wealthy visitors: smartly dressed businessmen, gorgeous society ladies, a tribe of Polynesian nationals in their colorful native garb. Cord followed a hallway to 503 and handed the key to the vigilante who'd led them there.

"Open it," he said.

The young man nodded eagerly and bent to unlatch the door. He was turning the knob when McGee planted his size-fourteen boot on the seat of his trousers and propelled him forward. The man sprawled across the threshold of the elegant suite as Cord and McGee entered nonchalantly behind him.

"I hear you're looking for us," said Cord.

Facing him were three men and a woman, seated more or less evenly around a large table of imported walnut. One of the men was Robert Murchison, the merchant who'd purchased McGee's pepper hours earlier. The other two were strangers to Cord, but the woman he knew very well.

"Cord Diamondback!" she said, leaping to her feet. "I didn't know you'd come to San Francisco—or that you were mixed up in the Meyers case."

Cord smiled. The woman was Melissa Fallows, daughter of Billy Fallows, the man he was accused of killing. She and Cord had met after the massacre at

Old Bone; their relationship had been brief but intimate, ending when Melissa went to the bayside city to pursue a career in politics. She was the last person Cord had expected to confront here, but perhaps he could turn it to his advantage.

"What's the meaning of this, Melissa?" demanded one of the councilmen. "Do you know this . . . this ruffian?"

"He's a gentleman, Jake," said Melissa firmly, combing back a stray lock of her butter-colored blond hair. "He tried to help in the ambush, when Uncle Dale was killed. Maybe he can help us now."

"Not likely," said Jake, sneering. He was tall and gray-haired, with a striking silver mustache. "Mars had the right idea in the first place. Let's find out what they know and then toss them out on their backsides. Half-witted meddlers we don't need, especially now."

"He's right, you know," said another councilman, a stout man with pale eyes and watery lips. "The sooner they're out of here, the happier I'll be."

Cord frowned at him. "Mr. Mars, I presume."

"Heywood Mars," said the stout man, nodding. "Think of me when you're crossing the state line out of here—after you've told us all you know of Deborah Meyers and her ill-fated fiancé."

Cord fingered the butt of his Schofield. "You're not in a good bargaining position, Councilman. Most of your hoodlums are decorating the floor of a downtown saloon—not that our brawl settled anything. Maybe it's time we sat down and talked out our differences in a more civilized setting."

Jake and Mars started to interrupt, but Murchison cut them off with a wave of his white-gloved hand. "Let's hear him out," said the dockside merchant.

"Mr. Diamondback is . . . uh . . . a very resourceful man."

"Thank you," said Cord. He pulled a straight-back chair from the corner and straddled it, putting himself between Melissa and Jake. McGee remained standing.

"Here's what we know," Cord began, choosing his words carefully. Laying his cards on the table seemed the right move, since it would consolidate Melissa's confidence in him and might tempt the others to offer more information. Briefly, he outlined what he knew of Deborah's disappearance, and the rumors of her fiancé's fleeing the plague ship.

Melissa took up the story when he finished. "You've got to most of it already, Cord," she explained. "Deborah did go to Rheingold, and apparently saw him before he died. We wanted to put her under quarantine because of her exposure, but she vanished before we found her. She's probably dead in an alley somewhere." Melissa touched his sleeve. "I'm sorry, Cord."

Cord felt little grief for a girl he'd never met, but he knew how wrenching the news would be to Victoria. No way of telling it would be gentle enough, but that was a problem for another time. "You mentioned another problem, Melissa. What is it?"

Melissa exchanged glances with Heywood Mars. Mars licked his lips and looked around at the others uncertainly. Finally, he shrugged and said, "Might as well tell him."

"All right." Melissa faced Cord. "The plague ship has arrived. Last night the *Orpheus* came into San Francisco Bay, with not one member of the crew left alive. A tug towed it to a remote section of the harbor, but so far no one's had the nerve to board it and investigate. We're thinking of setting fire to it."

"Like hell!" said Mars, quivering with indignation. "That's *my* boat, young lady, and no one's destroying it without finding out what happened. If one plank of the *Orpheus* is damaged, I'll expect this damned city to pay for it!"

"*You* should pay *us*," said Murchison. "For the damage a plague scare will surely cause our city. For the loss of life, loss of commerce, and loss of civic pride in a city threatened by contagion. Your ship, sir, poses a hazard to the commonwealth that may be decades in correcting."

"Send me a bill," said Mars.

For several moments no one spoke. Mars and Murchison glared at each other; Jake seemed to favor Mars's position, but only marginally, and Melissa supported neither. Finally, Cord cleared his throat.

"Sounds like you could use a judge," he observed.

Jake and Mars looked puzzled, but Murchison groaned. "I've had enough of your decisions to suit me, Cord. Twenty minutes after my purchase this morning a clipper came in with enough pepper to spoil the market—along with any profits I might have realized. I suppose you'll claim you didn't know the other ship was coming."

"Of course I knew," Cord said frankly. "But the decision was a fair one. You set a price, and got it— not a penny more than you asked to pay. What's fairer than that?"

Murchison rubbed his temple. "How would you approach *this* problem?"

"Carefully. For one thing, no one seems to know just what happened out there. I need more information before a verdict can be rendered. With the permission of Mr. Mars, I'd like to board the *Orpheus* and find out what I can."

"But it's a plague ship!" Melissa protested. "You could be infected! You could die!"

Cord held Murchison's eye. "You asked me what I'd do, and I'm telling you. One thing: I'd want a physician to come with me, a specialist if possible, to identify the cause of death of those crewmen."

"But that's preposterous!" said Murchison. "No doctor would agree to—"

"Carpenter would do it," Melissa broke in. "To him that ship is a floating laboratory. And I've never known him to worry about himself, if there was knowledge to be had."

"But who would sail you out there? Who would dare?"

"I would," said Beefeater McGee. "Cord and me, we're in this together."

Melissa nodded soberly. "It appears we have a strategy, gentlemen. Unless there are any objections, Mr. Murchison?"

Murchison glowered at her, but said nothing. The others were just as reticent, so Melissa turned to Diamondback. "Looks like you're working for us, Cord. What's your standard fee?"

"Five thousand ought to cover it," said Cord thoughtfully.

"Five *thousand?*" cried Murchison. "How in hell do you expect us—" He broke off as someone knocked on the door, three times. McGee spun around, ready for a fight.

"It's the mayor," said Melissa. "He said he'd stop by to see what we've decided. Let him in, Captain."

McGee nodded and opened the door. Behind it was an impeccably dressed man with salt-and-pepper hair and a swift sure smile—although it seemed a bit hollow during the current crisis. Cord sensed a bedrock of wisdom and real compassion behind the bland smile he presented to the world.

"What's the consensus?" he asked Melissa.

"We've hired this man to help," said the council-woman, gesturing at Cord. "Cord Diamondback, Mayor Howard Wylie."

"Pleased to meet you," said the mayor, taking Cord's hand. "I'm sure Melissa's confidence will be well placed." He turned back to the doorway. "Please come in, Becky. I want you to meet someone."

Cord frowned. "Your wife is here?"

"Of course—"

The mayor's wife stood in the doorway, her eyes fixed on Cord. She made no move to greet him. Her expression was one of stark horror, a woman afraid beyond words, face to face with her single greatest fear.

"It's *him!*" she cried, pointing a trembling finger at Cord Diamondback. "From the bedroom, that night with Billy Fallows, it's the murderer—*Christopher Deacon!*"

# 9

Cord frowned, showing curiosity but nothing else. Rebecca Wylie had been there at Billy Fallows's murder, and her identification was unqualified—but Cord feigned innocence, because he could think of nothing else to do.

"I'm afraid I don't understand," he said.

"*Murderer!*" hissed Rebbeca Wylie, backing away from him. "You killed him, you son-of-a-bitch! They should hang you right here!"

Cord watched the mayor for his reaction. It wasn't what he expected. Instead of responding with shock and amazement, or gaping at Cord with stunned disbelief, he took his wife's hand in both of his own.

"You have to calm down, dear," he said soothingly. "I know you're upset, but please try to stay calm. Would you like some of your medicine?"

Rebecca looked from him to Cord, and back again. "I don't want any medicine! It's him, Howie—the murderer, from that night in the bedroom. You've got to believe me."

Howard stroked his wife's hair. "You said it was him in the theater, dear—and before that, in Chinatown. There's no end to it, is there? Everywhere you look you see the face of Christopher Deacon."

Robert Murchison coughed awkwardly. Heywood Mars shuffled some papers. The mayor touched his wife's cheek and pointed solemnly at Cord.

"Take a good look now," he said gently. "A close look. Study him as carefully as you can."

Rebecca looked at Cord, still white with fear. Cord gave her his very best smile. Gradually, the panic fled Rebecca's features, like the passing of a feverish delirium.

"Honestly, now," said the mayor, "is this *really* the man you saw on that terrible night?"

Rebecca looked away. "I guess not."

"All right, then." Howard sighed. "Why don't you go down to the carriage and wait for me? This won't take very long."

Rebecca nodded and left. Howard turned to Cord and said quietly, "I'm sorry. She's been like that for more than three years now. She was there when Christopher Deacon attacked Senator Fallows, and she's never come to grips with it. I only hope someday the doctors can help her."

"So do I," said Cord, feeling a twinge of real guilt.

Rebecca had been an inadvertent victim of that night's violence; Cord had meant her no harm, but her trauma had been beyond his control. He shook his head and reminded himself how necessary his vengeance was.

Melissa cleared her throat. "In any case," she said, forcing the conversation back to the business at hand, "we wish to hire Mr. Diamondback for an investigation of the plague ship—and to render a decision as to what damages should be paid, and what action should be taken. With your permission, Mr. Mayor—"

"Just a minute," said Murchison angrily. "Why not mention this man's fee—if the term applies to such a flagrant misuse of funds? Mr. Mayor, this is the greatest swindle since Honest Harry Meiggs looted the treasury and fled to South America!"

"What is his price?" asked Wylie.

"Five thousand dollars!" cried Murchison.

Mayor Wylie studied Diamondback with a practiced eye. "Melissa seems to trust you," he observed. "And her approval doesn't come easily. Gentlemen, I suggest we take the councilwoman's advice and hire this man for the requested fee. Anyone who can shed light on this sordid affair is worth retaining at any price."

He turned abruptly and headed for the door. He was almost out it when he paused and turned back. "Mr. Diamondback?"

"Yes?"

"Please understand that my wife is no lunatic. Aside from this one irrational fear, she is sensible, and sane, and the finest wife a man could ask for." He studied the floor. "It's well known that she was having an affair with Fallows on the night of the murder. I've often wondered if her real fear isn't that I'd leave her over it, even today. Hard to tell, I guess."

He left without waiting for an answer.

"So now you know, Judge," said Heywood Mars derisively. "The mayor's wife is a fruitcake, and the old boy isn't far behind her. But what do you care? You're making money off it, right?"

Cord ignored him, addressed Melissa. "How about it? Am I hired?"

"Well . . . if there are no further objections . . ."

No one spoke. Melissa nodded; on a sheet of hotel stationery she wrote the name and address of the doctor they'd chosen to help Cord. Under it she wrote her own address, and signed it with a flourish. Cord took the folded sheet, smiled, and followed Beefeater McGee out the door.

"I still don't get it," said McGee. "What's the sawbones gonna do for us?"

"Identify the disease, for one thing," Cord explained. They were on horseback, crossing Portsmouth Square. A pedestrian glared at Cord, giving his horse a wide berth. "For another, make sure it was the disease that killed them. If I'm to make a fair decision, I need to know everything."

"Suit yourself," said the captain. "Where's this place again?"

"On Grant Street. We're almost there."

Cord and McGee kept riding, past the Hall of Justice and the El Dorado Saloon. The streets were crowded with riders, pedestrians, and carriages, briskly going about their business. Once in a while traffic would come to a standstill as the Clay Street cable car came through; it was a brightly painted passenger car pulled by underground cables. It was stuffed with passengers, sitting, standing, clinging to the handrails. Others ran alongside.

"Here it is," said Cord.

Before them was a one-story office building, butted against its neighbors on either side, with a hand-painted sign that read DENNIS CARPENTER, GENERAL PHYSICIAN, REASONABLE PRICES. Cord and McGee tied their horses to a post, and Cord rapped smartly on the door. After a moment it flew open and Dr. Dennis Carpenter said, "Yes? Can I help you?"

"Melissa Fallows recommended you," said Cord.

Carpenter's eyes narrowed. He was a short, intense man, with whitening hair and steel-rimmed glasses.

His eyes flicked from Cord to McGee and back again, like a card sharp eyeing his poker buddies. Finally, he stepped back and said, "Come in, please."

Both men stepped into an office crammed with notes and books and anatomical drawings. On a table in the center of the room was a wooden rack holding dozens of test tubes, all filled with exotic colored liquids. Beside it was a strange contraption that Cord recognized as an adjustable microscope. A glass slide rested in the specimen clips, and a notebook lay open beside it.

Carpenter moved some clutter from two overstuffed chairs and waved Cord and McGee into them. Then he sat down himself, on a workbench by the microscope. "So what does Melissa want now?"

"She wants to know if the city is faced with a plague epidemic," said Cord. Briefly, he explained about the ill-fated raft, and the suspected plague ship that had followed it. Carpenter nodded thoughtfully, tapping his teeth with a fountain pen.

"I wish I could have examined the bodies of Rheingold and the others," said Carpenter. "By now they'll have been cremated, of course, but the ship itself should provide the clues we need. Have any bodies been removed for study?"

"No one's going near it. They're afraid to risk infection."

"I don't blame them." Carpenter laid his pen aside. "How much do you know about the plague, Mr. . . ."

"Cord Diamondback. And I know a few things." He ticked them off on his fingers. "The disease is transmitted by rats, notably the black rats common in ships and houses. It spreads from rats to people by flea bites. Once infected, a person suffers fever, shaking chills, and delirium, usually followed by death from blood poisoning."

"Most impressive," said Carpenter. "Are you a doctor, as well?"

"No, he's not," McGee broke in. "But the plague interests him."

"So it seems. One thing you didn't mention, though, is the greatest danger of all. Infection from rat fleas is hardly sufficient to explain history's worst epidemics, like the Black Death that claimed twenty-four million Europeans in the fourteenth century. No, that takes a deadlier contagion."

Carpenter peered into his microscope, shook his head, changed slides. "Pneumonic plague," he said. "Clinically, it's similar to the bubonic type, but it doesn't take flea bites to get it. Just breathe the same air as a plague victim. Pretty soon your lungs are infected, the germs multiply, and every cough sprays them in all directions." He pushed his glasses up on his nose. "Still want to check out that ship?"

Cord looked at McGee. The bearded captain rubbed his hands together and said, "Sure thing, Doc. I like a little risk now and then. Keeps me from getting bored."

"Me, too," said Cord. "Are you ready to join us, Doctor?"

"Hold it, now," said Carpenter, raising his hands. "I haven't said I'd do it. This isn't a stroll through Golden Gate Park, you know."

Cord remembered Melissa's words about the doctor's obsession with knowledge. "Aren't you curious about that ship? Wouldn't you like to find out what really happened?"

"Sure I would. I'm just not sure it's worth getting dead over."

"Well, how would you approach the problem—if you *did* go on board?"

"Hmm." Carpenter rubbed his chin. "Several ways, probably. Examine the bodies for classic plague symptoms—enlarged glands in the neck and groin, congestion in the lungs, submucosal hemorrhage. Blood samples could be checked for septicemia, and lymph nodes for pus formation and leukocytes. Then, of course, I'd look for subepithelial hemorrhaging and fibrin deposits in skin lesions—"

"Then you'll do it," said Cord.

"I will?"

"Yes. Because it's the perfect test of your clinical skills, and you can't bear the thought of an unsolved pathogenic riddle. I think you'll risk your life rather than let it go unexamined, unsolved."

Carpenter flushed in spite of himself, obviously pleased with Cord's assessment. "Maybe you're right," he admitted, reaching for his medical bag. "I'd better come along, just to see for myself." He thrust some equipment into the bag. "Sure wish I had more sense, though."

# 10

"That's the plague ship," said Beefeater McGee, pointing just ahead. "You folks still want to board her?"

Cord braced himself against the forward rail of McGee's small schooner and studied the vessel just ahead of them. The foundering clipper bore the legend ORPHEUS, and seemed quite seaworthy—but it was unnaturally still for a ship anchored in harbor. Cord could smell the sour tang of rotten meat, even at a distance of several hundred feet.

"We've come this far," said Cord. "Shame to waste the trip."

Beside him, Dennis Carpenter's features were tight with tension. The doctor had hardly spoken as McGee sailed them to the secluded part of the bay where the *Orpheus* was anchored. Now he looked up and said carefully, "Would anyone like a couple of tablets for nausea? Besides me, I mean."

"Relax, Doc," said McGee, making a fine adjustment to the mainsail. "We'll just hop on and take a quick look around. They'll hardly know we were there. Ain't that right, Cord?"

"Suits me," said Diamondback. By now the *Orpheus*'s deck was plainly visible, as the ship bobbed fitfully in the harbor tide. The deck was covered with human bodies, frozen in every ghastly posture: lying, crawling, thrashing in anguish. Some had been struggling to hurl themselves overboard. One man's throat had been ripped open for no apparent reason.

Cord felt a touch of fear as he noticed something else: the bodies were not at rest. They were jerking, twitching, rolling from side to side, as if the spirits of the dead men were fighting to reclaim them. But that was superstitious nonsense; the crewmen were dead, stiff and cold as slabs of butchered beef.

They seemed to move because they were covered head to foot with rats.

Cord watched as a furry black beast scampered over the chest of a fallen seaman, seeking the soft folds of his throat. The rat sank its teeth into the sailor's neck, bloodying its fur with a dribble of bright red, pressing in for another bite. Others smelled the blood and hurried to join him.

"Now we know how it was spread around," said Cord grimly. "Those rats must have multiplied in the hold—and the plague along with them. Before long, the whole boat was a death trap. The crewmen never had a chance."

"Excuse me," said Carpenter. He put three tablets in his mouth and washed them down with a cupful of bottled water. Then he took a sterile cloth, doused it with alcohol, and tied it over his nose and mouth. "You boys should do the same," he said.

Cord shrugged and followed Carpenter's example, but McGee wouldn't hear of it. "You want me to worry about the *air?* Forget it, Doc. I'm not scared of anything I can't see."

"A pity," said Carpenter.

McGee brought his boat in beside the luckless

clipper. There was an audible thump as the hulls collided, and McGee tied them together with a length of stout rope. "After you," he said, boosting Cord up over the *Orpheus*'s side rail.

The stench was unbearable. Cord fought the urge to vomit as a rat dropped the finger it was chewing and rushed over to sniff at his boot. He kicked it aside and trampled it, breaking its neck under his heel. The other rats ignored him, busily scavenging the dead crewmen.

"Armageddon," said Carpenter, his voice muffled by the face mask. "And less than a hundred yards from the busiest port of the West Coast. Do you have any idea what would happen if the plague got loose here? How far it would travel? How many would die?"

"Do what you have to," said Diamondback. "I'm going below."

The doctor shook his head. "You're a bigger fool than I realized, Cord. And that's going some, believe me." He shuddered and crouched by one of the bodies, opening his medical bag.

Cord pulled open a door leading downward, then had to back away from the suffocating smell. A body lay sprawled on the stairway, grasping for the door with a fingerless hand. From below came the chittering of still more rats, amplified by the ship's interior.

"What's down there, Cord?" asked Beefeater McGee.

Cord shrugged. "Hard to say from up here." He started down the steps, warily skirting the dead crewman, picking his way into the gloom. At the base of the stairs was a kerosene lantern, hung on a nail. Cord fumbled a match from his pocket and fired the lantern, feeding the wick until a dull glow lit up the hold.

A tight circle of rodent eyes stared back at him.

Cord swung the lamp around, forcing the rats to back off. Cautiously, he started forward, with McGee following. Crates and barrels lined the sides of the hold; Cord reached the nearest barrel and tapped it with his knuckles. "Liquid contents, half full," he decided. "Probably a wine barrel."

"What's the next one?" asked McGee.

Cord sniffed the air. Under the stench of foul bodies was a second odor, more agreeable. "Almonds," he said, prying open the next barrel. It was indeed filled with almonds, a welcome relief from the putrid smells filling the rest of the hold.

Working quickly and carefully, Cord and McGee inspected the remaining contents of the cargo hold. All told, there were three barrels of almonds, two crates of tropical fruit, four wine barrels, and two hundred pounds of exotic spices. There was also a barrel of pepper, something sure to infuriate Murchison if McGee was tactless enough to mention it.

"And that's about it," said McGee, as the last items were tallied. "Not too exciting, I guess, but it was worth looking. You want to get out of here now?"

Cord glanced around, spotting something on the interior wall. "Not yet, McGee. Have a look at this."

He held the lantern up to a broken locker, with CAPTAIN MICHAELS painted above it. The locker door was jammed shut, but Cord pulled with all his strength and the broken door snapped outward. Cord held his lamp up to the locker's interior, searching intently for clues.

What he found was confusing. First was a hard-bound copy of Charles Darwin's controversial book,

*On the Origin of Species,* and a report describing the work of a monk named Gregor Mendel. Under these was the *Orpheus*'s cargo manifest, which Cord folded and stuck into his pocket.

"Very interesting," said McGee drearily. "You ready to go yet?"

"Almost." Cord was turning away when he noticed a crumbly, greenish powder at the foot of the broken locker. He knelt and took it between his fingers, feeling its texture. The powder was a leafy residue, fibrous and brittle, from a plant once kept there and now removed.

But why?

He was pondering the problem when a hoarse cry echoed from the topside. McGee muttered "What the hell—?" and hurried to join Cord, who was already bounding up the stairs three at a time.

At the head of the stairs Cord paused to get his bearings. The cry had come from Carpenter, and it was obvious what he'd yelled about: a new ship had arrived, a clipper bearing no legend or identifying markings of any kind. Grim-faced men poured off the clipper onto McGee's boat, moored alongside.

"I don't know who they are, or what they want," said Carpenter anxiously, eyeing the strange vessel. The doctor had set up his microscope on a wooden stool, and was studying a tissue sample carved from the nearest crewman. "But I have the feeling they're not friendly."

"Let's ask them," said Cord, tearing off his mask. He peered over the gunwale, then ducked back as a .45 slug whined off the hull. "Maybe you're right," he admitted, drawing his Schofield.

"Well, I'm not happy about them being here, either," said McGee, pulling a Remington .44 from his belt. Boldly, he stood up and fired three rounds into the intruder's midst, winging one and scattering the rest. Before Cord could stop him, he vaulted over the rail and crashed down onto the foredeck of his schooner, sending its other end high into the air. Two intruders toppled from the stern into the cold, frothing water.

Cord leaped after McGee onto the schooner's deck, but McGee was already up and firing. The captain picked off two of them before a stray bullet caught him in the shoulder and sent him crashing to the deck, moaning in pain. Cord sent a bullet through the windpipe of the nearest assailant, then fired two more at his companions. One clutched his hip and tumbled sideways into the water.

The unmarked clipper pulled free of McGee's craft and set sail to evade them, slicing through the waves. Cord took aim at the retreating craft and steadied his gun, using a double-handed grip. Before he could fire, something whistled through the air and struck his hand. The Schofield bounced off the deck into the sea.

Cord's hand was suddenly numb and cold. He looked down and saw why. A six-pointed throwing star was embedded in the back of his hand, between the second and third knuckles. One of its points protruded from his palm. Cord ducked behind the wheelhouse, trying to get the star out of his hand without slicing a tendon.

He was still trying when the death scream of Dr. Dennis Carpenter echoed across the bay.

# 11

Cord would never forget that scream. It was a cry of such terror that for an instant he froze against the cabin, wondering what on God's earth could inspire such fear. He thought of trapped animals, dying children, victims of incurable madness.

Then the scream broke off, all at once, like a flame plunged in water. Cord listened for other sounds and heard nothing. McGee lay on the deck where he'd fallen, stretched out like a sleeping buffalo.

Cord's hand hurt like hell.

He gripped the throwing star with the thumb and forefinger of his good hand and pulled hard. For an anguished moment it wouldn't move. Then it slid a fraction, slowly, painfully—until suddenly it jerked free, dappling the deck with blood spots.

McGee said something unintelligible and rolled over, leaving his Remington on the deck planks. Cord snatched up the revolver in his good hand and peered over the side of the *Orpheus*. Dr. Carpenter was dead, a rumpled heap of flesh and clothing next to an upended microscope. Behind him was the Grim Reaper himself.

Cord rubbed his eyes, fighting a sudden sick wooziness. It wasn't the Reaper. The Reaper was a product of superstitious awe, a phantasm found only in the campfire tales of easily frightened greenhorns. The lithe, black-garbed figure bent over Carpenter's body was no more a ghost than Diamondback himself.

Cord blinked at the ebon shape, studying the perfect physique, the clean economy of movement. The man was almost wraithlike, wasting not a gesture as he straightened from Carpenter's body and turned to face Cord. Only his eyes were visible, over a shroud of black silk. The eyes were as colorless as Cord's own, but with no trace of compassion.

Cord fired. The shot was an easy one, but the ghost figure ducked aside and Cord's bullet slammed into the mast behind him. Cord tracked the man with his gunsight, firing again and again. His speed was unbelievable. Every shot cleft the air behind him, leaving its mocking target intact.

Cord wondered if the man was impervious to bullets. Once, in Santa Fe, he'd heard a man brag that he couldn't be shot because he was protected by Satan himself. That man was dead now, killed within minutes of his fatal boast—but the dark figure in his gunsight was still alive, and had no right to be.

Cord fired again, and missed.

Then it was over. The ghost man leaped off the boat, knifing into the water. Cord dropped his gun and slumped against the side rail. The water was still, undisturbed by the killer's escape.

Carpenter—he had to help Carpenter. Cord boosted himself back up onto the *Orpheus*, wincing at the pain in his hand. The rail was slick and warm where he grabbed it, and Cord realized he was still bleeding. He wrapped his hand in his shirt and stumbled toward Carpenter.

The doctor was not dead. He was lying in a puddle

of his own spilled blood, and Cord could see a sodden lump of tissue that might have been intestine. But Carpenter was speaking. "Not so hard," he said tonelessly. "Knew I'd figure it out."

Cord crouched by his side. "Lie back, Doctor," he said, thinking how nice it would be to take his own advice. "Don't try to speak . . ."

"Not so hard," Carpenter repeated. "Just . . . had to name . . . the compound. Prussic acid. That's it, prussic . . . acid." He closed his eyes and lay back against the planks. "How'd I do?"

Cord took his wrist, felt for the pulse. There wasn't any. Carpenter was at peace, and it was frightfully tempting to lie down and join him. But he had other things to do . . .

"Wake up, McGee," said Cord, jostling the big captain with his boot. "We're coming into the harbor."

"Huh?" McGee tried to sit up, then winced as the pain hit his shoulder. "Christ, I'm *hurt*. What'd you wake me up for?"

"Need help bringing the boat in. You're not hurt that bad, I've seen you spear a whale with your arm in an elbow cast. I figure the exercise will do you good."

McGee groaned and rubbed his neck. "Where's Carpenter?"

"In the cabin. He's dead. I couldn't help him."

"Damn! I kinda liked that little fella." McGee looked into the cabin and yelped with surprise. "Hey! There's *two* bodies in here!"

"I know. The other's a gunman, the only dead one that didn't fall overboard. I searched his body for clues."

"What'd you find?"

"Not much." Cord adjusted the rudder as the wharf

pilings loomed before them. "Help me trim the sail, would you?"

Cord and McGee brought the small schooner in and tied it to a dock piling, working together with a swift precision they'd developed years ago. Cord could almost believe they were back on the high seas, chasing down whales—and the sordid business of Fallows's murder and the plague threat were only troubling daydreams. For a moment it was hard to believe otherwise.

But the moment ended when they stepped onto the Jackson Street wharf and found Councilman Jake Jennings waiting for them. Jake was the councilman with the silver mustache, opposed to hiring Cord. He was waiting with his arms sternly folded, looking even more impatient than usual.

"About time you returned," he snapped, looking pointedly at his watch. "I trust you enjoyed your little jaunt around the harbor, since you were traveling at our expense. I also trust you never made it to the *Orpheus*—or, if you did, that you didn't stay long enough to acquire any useful information."

Cord shrugged and started past him. Jennings rushed over to block his way. "Am I right?"

"Maybe," said Cord. "I don't know yet."

"So you admit that your trip was an utter waste of money and time?"

"All depends. You'll have to read my report." Cord started past him again.

Jennings grabbed his shoulder. "How much time have you wasted?"

"How long have we been talking?"

"Look, I'll put it to you straight. For this job you get five thousand dollars, right?" Jennings reached into his coat pocket and extracted a checkbook, made of hand-tooled leather. He scribbled out a check and gave it to Cord. "Here's ten thousand. Get lost. This city can handle its own problems."

Cord tucked the check back into Jennings's pocket. "Sorry to put you off, Councilman," he said briskly, "but I've got work to do. Come on, McGee."

He brushed past Jennings, ignoring the councilman's objections, and was halfway down the wharf before Jennings yelled, "Hey! Where's Carpenter?"

"In the boat!" Cord yelled back. "He's the one on the bottom!"

Jennings opened his mouth, and closed it again.

Cord and McGee reclaimed their horses and worked their way through the wharfside crowd. The smell of broiled seafood was everywhere as dinner time approached, and restaurant-goers jostled for a place in line outside the city's finest eateries. Cord picked out the smells of steamed oysters and freshly baked bread.

"Where to?" asked McGee. "You want to go see that lady lawyer again?"

"Not yet," Cord decided. He wasn't anxious to give Victoria the sad news about her daughter—especially unconfirmed. "No, I've got another plan, McGee. But it'll have to wait until dark."

"Suits me," said the captain. "What'll we do until then?"

Cord grinned. "I expect we'll think of something."

"How come I never heard of this place?" asked Cord, frowning at the battered sign. Thick black letters said CACTUS BREATH CONNERY'S over a painted caricature of a man with arched eyebrows and a curly waxed mustache. The front door had a dent in it that was about the size of someone's head.

"You'll like it here," said McGee, selecting a

corner table. "The liquor's good, the girls are friendly, and the drinks are so cheap you'll give out before your money does. Paradise, if you ask me."

Cord grinned. "You always did have strong tastes, McGee. You remember the night we got drunk at Spider Kelly's?"

"And the crimps tried to shanghai us? Sure." McGee shook his head. "Poor fellas. I hope the big guy's neck got better."

"Hey, what you boys drinkin'?" asked a busty barmaid. She carried an arsenal of mixed drinks on a cork tray. "Hurry up, I got three girls and a fat guy waitin' at the next table."

Cord shrugged. "Two Scotches, no ice."

"And two for me," said McGee. "Tell me about this plan of yours, Cord."

"Well, it's kind of a long shot," Cord admitted. "It occurred to me while I was searching the dead gunman's clothing."

"I thought you didn't find anything."

"I didn't find much. His pockets were empty of all identification. But his shirt was white silk, a kind I haven't seen before."

"So?"

"This was sewn into the back of his collar." Cord fished in his pocket, pulled out an embroidered tag. On the tag was a picture in threads of red and gold, showing a dragon biting its tail. "This shirt was made in a factory in Chinatown—a factory with its own distinctive label. If we can find the place and search it, it's a good bet we'll get some clues to who sent those harbor pirates—and why."

McGee nodded thoughtfully. He was about to comment when the barmaid laid two glasses in front of him, and two more in front of Cord. Diamondback gave her a bill and joined McGee in his first Scotch.

"You think that'll work, Cord?" asked McGee, savoring the warm liquid.

"Beats me," said Cord. "Maybe Jennings was right; maybe it's an utter waste of time. But it's the best idea I've got." He raised his glass. "To Chinatown—and the redoubtable Mr. Jennings."

They touched glasses, and drank. Soon they were ready for refills, and the barmaid did a brisk business between them, the three ladies, and the fat man. Cord had stopped counting Scotches when McGee looked over and said, "Hey! There's someone who might help us!"

"Who?" Cord looked in the same direction and saw two men in trail-worn clothes, talking animatedly with a nattily dressed Chinaman. One of the cowboys kept slamming his fist into the table, slopping whiskey over the edge of his glass.

McGee gulped his latest Scotch and stood up, beckoning Cord to follow. Both men crossed the bar in time to catch some fragments of the argument between the cowboys and the Chinaman.

"For the last time," the fist-slamming cowboy was saying, "I don't *want* another girl. I want Sue Lee Kwan, and I mean to get her."

"She not in business anymore," said the Chinaman helplessly. "She and other client fall in love, get married, raise small ones. Find other girl, no trouble."

The cowboy's hand went to his gun belt. "Forget it, laundryman. I want to see Sue Lee Kwan, and if she's married she'll just have to get *un*married!" Angrily, he drew his gun—or started to. Before he could get it clear of the holster, Cord drove his knuckles into the soft spot behind the man's ear. He said "Unff" and fell nose first into the tabletop.

The other cowboy was too surprised to draw his gun. McGee gripped the front of his shirt in one hand, lifted him out of his chair, and said, "Mind if we use your table, son?"

"Uh . . . no . . . help yourself," said the second man, goggling at McGee's lumberjack fist. Cord noticed that the man's boots were well above the floor. McGee set him down and said, "Much obliged," as the hapless cowboy darted for the exit.

Cord tipped the other one out of his chair, relieving him of his gun as he fell. "Man shouldn't carry one of these if he can't use it," Cord observed.

"What honorable fellows want here?" asked the Chinaman.

"First you can knock off the stupid talk," said McGee. "Do we look like a couple of hayseeds?"

"Looks not matter—sorry, force of habit." He grinned. "What do you boys need?"

"That's better. Cord, this here's Arnold Chan, sneakiest cuss I ever shared a bottle with. You want to know anything about Chinatown, he's the guy to ask. Bastard's a walking news service."

"For a price," said Chan.

Cord showed him the embroidered label. "Try this one, Chan. Where's this from? I want to know the address of the manufacturer."

Chan eyed the label for a fraction of a second. "Couldn't tell you for less than fifty bucks. Association rules, you know."

"I'll give you thirty."

"Thirty-five."

Cord slapped three bills on the table and waited.

Chan palmed them in one swift motion and said, "Dragon's Tongue Garment Mill, Washington and Grant streets. Kung Lin Saw, proprietor. It's a meeting place for the On Leongs, so watch your step—we don't need another tong war."

"I'm not fond of them myself," said Cord. "One more question. Earlier today I saw a man dressed in black, head to foot, all except his eyes. He was so fast I couldn't shoot him at five yards. What's it cost to find out who he was?"

Chan shuddered visibly. "Nothing. On the house. I'll tell you and then you'll forget you ever saw me— and if you're smart, you'll forget *him*, too." Chan glanced over his shoulder. "He's a *ninja*, the best there ever was. Everyone's afraid of him, even white folks—because he's better at killing than they are. I knew someone who got on his kill list and committed suicide rather than face him."

"I'll risk it," said Cord. "What's his name?"

"No one knows, except his nickname—a name that suits him quite well. *Nightmare*."

Cord shrugged. "A little pretentious, isn't he? Couldn't he have picked a simpler name, like Yellow Dog or Gold Canary or something?"

"Not funny, Diamondback. Least of all to him. Nightmare is a master of the arts of combat, and he's not graceful about criticism. If you make him mad, he'll cut you up and barbecue the pieces."

"Life's a gamble," said Cord, standing up. "You coming, McGee?"

"Sure, what the hell." The captain joined Cord, pausing to grasp Chan's shoulder in a grip that made the Chinaman wince. "Not to sound ungrateful, Chan—we appreciate the help—but it'd be nice if you didn't spread this around for the next day or so, until we've given ourselves a proper introduction."

Arnold Chan looked hurt. "You helped me out tonight, friends. You think I'll sell you short? Honorable gentlemen not know of Chinese loyalty to debt partners."

"How about loyalty to a fast buck?" asked McGee. Before Chan could compose a suitably modest answer, the captain and Cord were gone.

# 12

"Damned if that little bastard wasn't right," said McGee, pointing just ahead.

He and Cord were at the corner of Washington and Grant streets, in the shadow of an elegant Chinese restaurant. Diagonally across from them was a massive building in need of a paint job; a sign over the doorway read DRAGON'S TONGUE GARMENT MILL, with a hand-painted picture of a dragon biting its tail. The building showed no life of any kind, and at that hour pedestrians were few and far between.

"So how do we get in?" asked McGee. "Me, I vote we break the door down. Of course, we could bust in the windows just as easily. Up to you, Cord."

"Let's take a closer look," said Diamondback. He crossed the street and pressed into an alley, beside the garment mill. The alley ran the length of the building and opened onto a sandlot, out of sight from the street. Facing the sandlot was the building's rear wall—with three darkened windows, chest-high.

"We'll go in here," Cord announced. "How's your shoulder?"

"Huh? Oh, it's just a pinprick, Cord." McGee lifted his arm and rotated it, wincing only slightly.

"Nothing a good fight won't fix up. How's your hand?"

Cord flexed his fingers. They were stiff, a little painful—but he could use a gun if he had to. The double-action .44 he'd taken from the drunken cowboy was a comforting weight in his holster.

"I'm fine," he said, examining the nearest window. It was casement type, not new, with six frosted panes and two clear ones. Cord pressed the bottom section experimentally and felt a slight give under his fingers.

"Want me to smash it open?" asked McGee, picking a rock out of the sandlot.

Cord shook his head. "I'd rather not announce our presence here. Besides, there's another way."

He pressed both hands against the edge of the lower window and pushed hard, careful not to break the glass. After several seconds the bottom section jumped its track and ground against the side jamb. Cord pushed harder and it fell inward. He caught it and lowered it to the floor.

Cord boosted himself up and scrambled inside, beckoning to McGee. The captain followed, hunching his mountainous shoulders to work them through the opening. Cord replaced the window section and tamped it back into its groove. "Now no one'll know we were here," he said.

The Dragon's Tongue Garment Mill stretched out around them. The mill was dark but the ceiling boasted a huge skylight, and they could see by the light of a three-quarter moon. What they saw were spinning wheels and steel power looms, some yards wide; the looms were driven by steam engine and fed from rollers of multicolored thread. Huge bins held bolts of woven fabric.

"What are we looking for?" asked McGee.

"Clues," Cord told him. "Get out there and find some."

McGee ambled halfheartedly through the semidarkness, poking at the silent machinery. Cord followed him, marveling at the intricate-weave patterns in the finished cloth. McGee tapped one of the big looms and said, "Nice, huh?"

"Nice, and efficient," said Cord. "Power looms are faster and cheaper than the hand-run models. This one was designed by William Crompton and his son, George, in a cotton factory in Massachusetts—"

"Tell me something," McGee broke in.

"Yes?"

"Is there anything you're *not* an expert on?"

Cord thought a moment. "Australian rugby scores. But don't spread it around."

McGee was framing his next comment when they came to a narrow, glass-paneled door. The door had a plate with the inscription KUNG LIN SAW. Cord tried it, found it unlocked, and let himself and McGee into a small office to one side of the work area.

The office was clean, sparsely furnished. An oak desk and chair stood by a lone filing cabinet, with one drawer standing open. On the desk was an ink-stained blotter with pictograms scribbled in the corners. Cord checked the open file drawer and found nothing but invoices and receipts, all in Chinese.

The other drawers were locked.

"Excuse me," said McGee. The captain took the open drawer in both hands, braced his foot against the cabinet, and pulled hard. The drawer tore loose from its moorings with the sound of breaking metal. Cord reached into the underlying drawer and felt something round and smooth.

"You found something?" asked McGee. "What is it?"

"Hard to say." Cord set the object on Kung Lin Saw's desk. It was a glass globe, heat-sealed, about the size of a balled fist. Inside was a culture plate with something greenish-gray growing on it.

"Let's take it with us," Cord decided. "I want this examined, by a doctor or a chemist. Maybe both. Melissa Fallows can recommend someone." He was stuffing the globe under his shirt when he noticed something: on its underside were two painted words in unreadable Chinese.

"Fix the drawer," said Cord, "so we can get out of here."

McGee stuffed the drawer back into its niche, vainly trying to make it look undisturbed. He and Cord made their way back into the factory proper, but they hadn't gone a dozen steps when a door slammed in the front of the building. Loud voices came closer, and footsteps—lots of them.

Cord and McGee retreated to Kung Lin Saw's office and watched through the glass panel. A cluster of Chinese came in and stationed themselves by one of the looms, glancing pensively around. All wore silk jackets with embroidered floral patterns. Soon they were joined by another group, and another. One man ran around with a box of strike-anywhere matches, lighting kerosene lanterns mounted on brackets in the wall.

"Nice timing, Cord," said McGee under his breath. "There must be three dozen of 'em out there. You want to rush out and surprise them, or you think we should warn 'em first?"

"I'm going to wait and watch," said Cord. "You want to surprise them, help yourself."

McGee glared at him, but said nothing. In the work area, the hushed babble of voices came to an abrupt halt as a door slammed in the front of the building. Cord twisted to see who was coming and recognized the new man instantly.

Nightmare.

"The Exalted One!" cried a man in a floral-print shirt, throwing himself at Nightmare's feet. "A thousand prayers of gratitude for your kindness in attending our humble ceremony, most gracious one."

Nightmare placed a foot between the man's shoulder blades and rested his weight there, pushing the supplicant face first into the ground. The man continued to mumble incoherent praises. Nightmare faced the next man in line and said, "Has he come yet?"

"The Master? No, Exalted One, I was not expecting—"

"Not the Master, fool," said Nightmare icily. "The Master is known only to me. I mean the traitor, the One Who Betrays. Tonight he comes here, to seal our contract."

"Ah, yes." The underling's head bobbed as if on a string. "He is expected, and soon. I trust the On Leongs will receive our customary retainer for providing—"

"You receive what I choose to give," Nightmare hissed. "Do not forget your place, small one. The deal is mine, the terms are mine. Your precious tong is a convenience to me, nothing more." His eyes seemed to darken behind the veil. "Take care not to overstep yourself, tiny man."

"But surely—Exalted One, we are the largest gang in this city. There are regulations to be met, standards to uphold. How shall I tell my superiors—"

Nightmare moved. Or, rather, he *shifted*, and in the

space of an instant the underling felt a bruising hand clenched tightly on his shoulder and four fingers sharp against his throat. "Tell your superiors this," he said. "Your size, your power, are nothing to me. If any among you denies my terms, he will be blinded the first day; castrated the second; desemboweled the third. Can I trust you to deliver this message?"

The underling started to nod, winced as the nails pricked his throat. "Y-yes, Exalted One," he whispered.

"Excellent." Nightmare released the man with a shove. He stumbled backward, tripped, and smacked painfully into the floor. Nightmare folded his arms and said, "The rest of you remain loyal?"

"Please to fuck yourself," said a voice from the rear.

Everyone turned to look at him, including Cord and McGee. The new man was wiry and slender, not muscular but perfectly poised, light on his feet. He stepped forward and said boldly, "Care to repeat threats, One Who Talks Good Fight?"

Nightmare allowed himself a thin smile. "You have courage. Uncommon courage. What is your name, foolish one?"

"I am called"—he smiled back—"Daybreak. Nightmare's end. I must confess gratitude to you, kind sir. Your death at my hands will grant me leadership of the On Leong tong."

"Leadership in hell," said Nightmare, the smile gone. He took one step forward. "Good-bye, fool."

Daybreak rushed him. He came in low, feinted left, delivered a right forearm smash to the side of Nightmare's head, and finished with a left diagonal thrust kick. Nightmare spun away from the kick, caught Daybreak's foot behind his back, and sent the man crashing into the side of a wastebin.

The wiry challenger scrambled to his feet, assuming the posture of defense. Blood dripped from his nose. Nightmare nodded briskly; he danced forward, slapped Daybreak's hand aside, smashed his face with an open palm, caught him in the groin with a left knee hook, and drove an elbow thrust into his throat. Daybreak backed away, gagging. Nightmare grabbed him by the hair and drove two fingernails into Daybreak's eyes.

"Blinded," he said.

Daybreak clutched his face, alternately whimpering and screaming. Nightmare hit him in the stomach, swept his legs out from under him, and leaped high in the air, landing full force on Daybreak's groin. There was a sickening splattering sound, and a darkening stain formed on the front of Daybreak's pants.

"Castrated," said Nightmare.

Daybreak made a sound never meant for human vocal cords, not unlike the death scream of Dr. Carpenter on the filthy planks of the plague ship. Nightmare knelt over him and stiffened the fingers of his right hand into a bladelike cutting weapon. Cord saw the lamplight gleaming off his fingertips; Nightmare had reinforced his fingernails with razor-edged cutting steel.

Wordlessly, the black-clad figure drove his hand nails first into Daybreak's quivering abdomen. Blood and bile shot upward like Texas crude from an oil strike. Nightmare tightened his fist and withdrew it, pulling a bloody mess of ruptured membranes out of Daybreak's body.

"Disemboweled," he said.

"Christ," McGee whispered, shaking his head. "Our boy's got a mean streak, don't he?"

"Rough childhood, perhaps," said Cord.

Nightmare stood up and addressed the others, making no effort to clean his hand. "I'll repeat my question," he said reasonably. "Do the rest of you remain loyal?"

Absolutely no one spoke. Nightmare stared at each of them in turn, silently daring them to follow their friend's doomed example. Finally, he relaxed and folded his arms, the picture of serenity. "This matter is settled, then. Is there further business to conduct?"

No one suggested any. Nightmare was still waiting peacefully when a voice from the doorway said, "My God! What did you do, you bloody savage?"

Nightmare smiled. "Ah, yes. He Who Betrays pays us the honor of a visit." He turned to address the new arrival, smiling with unpleasant courtesy. "Good evening, Mr. Jennings. I trust you are well this evening?"

Councilman Jake Jennings looked sick. He rubbed his neck and smoothed his silver mustache, not looking at the mess on the floor. "I want no part of this," he insisted. "We made a deal; I'm here to close it. I've got the money right here." Jennings pulled a yellow envelope from his breast pocket and handed it to Nightmare.

Nightmare pulled it out with his right hand, bloodying the money. "All here, Mr. Jennings. Please to accept our gratitude. I trust the girl was to your liking?"

"Yeah, fine," said the councilman. "We had to shut her up anyhow. Might as well get some fun out of her first, right?"

"Quite so," said Nightmare, "as befits the On

Leong—the Society for Tranquil Consciousness. But I sense your consciousness will be even more tranquil if you leave here and never return. Is this not so?"

"Damned right," said Jennings, turning to leave. "I never came here; I never saw you people. Goodbye."

Jennings was almost to the door when Nightmare said softly, "A moment, please."

White-faced, the councilman turned back. Nightmare savored his raw fear for a moment, then smiled.

"I merely wish to provide a receipt for your payment, Councilman," he said.

"Oh, I don't need a—"

"To refuse is to risk offending the On Leong—and, not incidentally, my humble self. Will you take our receipt?"

Jennings ran a finger under his collar. "Uh, sure, guess there's no harm in it."

"Excellent." Nightmare turned to a sallow-faced Chinaman standing close by. "Kung Lin Saw, please go to your office and draw up a receipt for this gentleman, quickly."

"Yes, Exalted One." King Lin Saw nodded and hurried over to his office, muttering praises under his breath. He started to unlock the door, realized it was already unlocked, and threw it wide open. Cord Diamondback and Beefeater McGee stood facing him, guns drawn.

"I knew this wouldn't be easy," said Cord.

# 13

"Nobody moves!" said Beefeater McGee, shoving Kung Lin Saw out the door and waving his .44 at the others. Cord stayed abreast of him, watching everyone but paying special attention to Nightmare. Jennings was gone. The On Leongs looked confused, uncertain of what to do.

Then Nightmare spoke.

"Welcome, Cord Diamondback, Beefeater McGee. I am pleased you could attend these proceedings."

"It *has* been fun," said Cord, edging toward the door. "We'll have to get together again sometime. Have a few drinks, talk vivisection—"

"Sorry," said Nightmare, taking a step forward, "but I'd like to talk now. And I'm afraid I must insist."

"We've got the guns," McGee reminded him.

Nightmare smiled. Cord marveled at how you *knew* he was smiling, even under the veil of black silk—and how you were just as certain of the cruelty and cunning behind those hidden features. Nightmare turned to address the crowd of On Leongs.

"All of you, please give me your attention," he said. "These men wish to leave, and I wish them not to. Your task is to stop them. Anyone who does not assist me will suffer a vengeance beyond imagining."

A murmur went through the crowd of Chinese. Several looked sick. Cord and McGee found their way blocked by a solid wall of tong members, unmoved by the threat of gunfire.

"Well, we tried it the polite way," said McGee, shrugging. "How many bullets in that gun, Cord?"

"Not enough. It won't work, McGee." Cord holstered his gun and looked pointedly at McGee's. After a moment the captain did likewise. Cord faced Nightmare and said, "What do you want from us?"

Nightmare smiled again. "A small favor, nothing more. You see, Diamondback, your name is not unknown to me. You are much respected, as an arbiter of disputes and—more significantly—as a bare-knuckled fighter. How much money did you earn from your last prizefight, Diamondback?"

Cord winced. "Enough to buy some bandages and an elbow splint."

"Most amusing. But this time I ask you to fight for something much dearer—your personal freedom, and that of your friend. Only through my defeat can you leave this building alive."

"If you're trying to prove you're a better fighter," Cord said reasonably, "I'll save you the trouble. You're a better fighter. I'd be crazy to go against you."

Nightmare smiled a small bow. "My thanks, Diamondback."

"You're welcome. Can we go now?"

"You may not." Nightmare came forward slowly, his eyes fixed on Diamondback. "Our business here is unfinished."

Cord realized that Nightmare had assumed attack

posture, knees bent, arms flexed, poised to strike in a dozen ways. Cord backed away, trying to figure his next move. Nightmare took another step, closing the gap between them.

"This is the end of your life," said Nightmare.

He lunged forward and dove the heel of his hand into Cord's jaw, easily dodging Cord's defenses. Nightmare laughed and followed the jab with a bruising right hook that exploded against Cord's skull. Cord backed away, scrambling to regain his bearings. Nightmare threw another punch and Cord blocked it, but just barely.

"I see your reputation does not do you justice," Nightmare observed. "A pity. Good-bye, Diamondback."

Nightmare swept in, putting the full force of his strength and speed into a cobra strike at Cord's neck. Cord spun away and took the blow on his shoulder, wincing as Nightmare's fingers gouged his upper arm. Another strike came closer, so close it nicked his Adam's apple, but Cord ducked and back-pedaled out of range, playing for time. He had to think, to plan, to pick a strategy before Nightmare tore his throat out. What could he do?

What would Nightmare expect him *not to do?*

His time was gone. Nightmare lunged forward, full of lethal confidence, determined to end it fast. He feinted left, struck right, a straight-fingered jab at Cord's windpipe. Cord turned his shoulder to take the blow—

—and leaned *into* it, not away from it.

Nightmare's fingers struck his shoulder and stuck there, embedded in Cord's flesh. The pain was incalculable but Nightmare was startled, off guard at last, and Cord threw a left cross that caught the point of Nightmare's jaw and lifted him into the air, staggering backward, windmilling to regain his balance.

Cord danced forward to press his advantage. Nightmare stumbled and went down, landing hard—but his leg whipped out in a perfect sweep kick, knocking Cord's legs out from under him. Cord rolled aside as Nightmare came for him, clawing at his eyes.

A steel fingertip cut a furrow in Cord's forehead. Cord smacked the hand away and scampered backward, shielding his face. He fetched up against a power loom and waited for the next assault. When Nightmare moved in to finish him, Cord caught his hands and held fast.

Nightmare was faster, more adept at striking, but Cord was the stronger man. He forced his silk-garbed enemy back, trying to pin him to the floor. Cord almost did it but his shoulder was bleeding too badly, the pain pulsed with every heartbeat, and Nightmare twisted sideways and broke free.

"Perhaps you are a worthy opponent after all," Nightmare conceded.

He punctuated his comment with a side thrust kick that caught Cord in the kidneys and almost sent him to the floor again. Nightmare followed with a hook kick to Cord's groin and an elbow smash to the base of his neck. Cord sank to his hands and knees, bracing to retaliate, but Nightmare backed away.

"Watch," he told the staring spectators, "and learn."

Nightmare took a running start. He dove for the floor, yards away from Cord, caught himself on one hand, and piked into the air for a full twisting somersault that brought him down hands first, fingers outstretched, in a plunging slice that should have severed Cord's backbone.

But Cord moved. At the final instant he threw himself aside, just enough for Nightmare to miss and slam both hands into the floor. Nightmare howled with pain as the reinforced fingernail of his left ring finger bent backward and snapped off at the cuticle line.

Cord stood up and butted his head into Nightmare's throat. Nightmare croaked and staggered aside. Cord rushed him, but Nightmare caught the front of his shirt and threw him bodily into the nearest wall. For an instant Nightmare had a perfect target, but he was tiring now, perceptibly slowing, and Diamondback moved first.

One of the wall lanterns was within his reach. He grabbed it, tore it free of its iron bracket, and heaved it in a long, looping throw. Nightmare ducked, but it wasn't meant for him; the lantern crashed into the edge of a fabric bin and set fire to the cloth inside.

"What madness—?" gasped Nightmare, but before he could finish, Beefeater McGee grasped the bottom of the bin and toppled it, spilling its flaming contents over the dry plank floor. Kung Lin Saw screamed and tried to stamp out a bolt of fabric with his foot.

Three enraged Chinamen rushed McGee. He grabbed one by the collar, lifted him off the ground, and swung him like a club, scattering the others. McGee laughed and sent his human weapon flying across the factory.

Gunshots pierced the commotion.

Cord spun around, drawing his gun. One of the On Leongs had a revolver and was blasting away at McGee. A stray bullet whined off a spinning wheel; another shattered the glass in Kung's office door. Cord sent a .44-caliber slug into the gunman's breastbone.

He fell on his face, tried to rise, couldn't. Cord looked around, planning his next move.

Nightmare was gone.

The On Leongs seemed undecided whether to tackle Cord and McGee, or flee the fight and the fire. Most were fleeing. But a handful stayed behind, grappling with McGee, and two more came at Cord—

Something hit his hand from behind, knocking the gun away. A strong, thick-muscled Chinaman jumped onto his back, trying to force him down. Cord dove for the floor, hunching his shoulders so the other man would hit first. The man slammed into the floor and stayed there. Flames spread across his floral-print shirt, charring and blistering the skin beneath it.

Cord recovered his gun, just in time to blast one of the On Leongs at point-blank range. The tong member crumpled backward, beating at the air. Another stopped in midstep, wheeled around, and bolted for the door.

Smoke was filling Cord's lungs, making him choke. "Let's go, McGee," he said hoarsely. "This place will be cinders in five minutes."

"Just a minute, Cord." McGee grabbed the last of the tong men by the shirt and pitched him head first into a power loom. Panicked, the man thrashed around, entangling himself in the warp and weft threads. McGee started the engine and the man was pulled bodily into the mechanism, jamming him between the batten and breastbeam. Bones snapped as the ratchet wheel strained to keep turning.

"I hate it when folks gang up on me," said McGee.

"How about getting burned alive?" asked Cord. "Do you like that better?"

"Well—"

He broke off as a section of the roof collapsed,

crashing to the floor six feet from where they were standing. Cord and McGee raced for the door, dodging flaming debris and the bodies of fallen tong members. They made it outside and stood panting in the street, watching smoke pour from the windows. Lights went on up the street. Someone yelled, "Get the volunteer fire department! Tell 'em to get their butts down here!"

"Let's get the horses and get out of here," Cord suggested.

"Suits me," said McGee. "But what then? Where do we go next?"

"We visit Melissa Fallows," said Cord. "I want to hear what she can tell us about Councilman Jake Jennings."

# 14

---

"You sure this is it?" asked McGee. He and Cord were reining in their horses in front of an unspectacular clapboard house on Bay Street, crammed between other homes that were equally shabby. Some of the houses had garbage piled in front of them. A vague smell of sewage hung in the air.

Cord shrugged. "It's not what I expected. Of course, Melissa's always been full of surprises."

They tied their horses to a crooked post and made their way to the front door. Cord was poised to knock when a bone-chilling roar filled the air, like the cry of a predatory jungle beast. It went on for half a minute and then stopped, just as suddenly, leaving an unnatural silence.

"What in *hell* was that?" McGee demanded. "It sounded like something from the jungles of Borneo. Christ! Did that come from *inside?*"

"What'd I tell you about surprises?" said Cord.

He rapped three times on the front door; presently it was opened by an elderly Chinese with shoulder-length white hair, dressed in a perfectly tailored suit.

"Can I help you?" he asked politely. His voice held no trace of an accent.

"Well, fancy that!" guffawed McGee. "A servant

in a place like this! Must really be rough in the butler business if he has to—"

"Shut up," said Cord, facing the servant. "We have to talk to Miss Fallows, right away. I'm sure she'll want to talk to us."

"Very well." The Chinaman directed them inside and led them down a dim, unpainted hallway. At its end was the study, a converted bedroom now filled with bookshelves, old legal volumes, and stacks of correspondence. Melissa Fallows sat in an overstuffed chair in the center of the room, scribbling on a legal pad.

"You have guests," said the Chinaman.

Melissa looked up in surprise. "Cord! Captain McGee! What are you doing here? Did you find out anything?"

"Just a bit," said Cord, sitting back against a rolltop desk. "For one thing, we found out Councilman Jennings is tied into the conspiracy."

Melissa raised an eyebrow and laid her pen aside. "You'd better tell me everything, Cord," she said carefully.

Cord summarized their investigation, leaving out nothing. In the course of their last encounter, Cord had grown to trust Melissa, in spite of her bloody family history. He admired her for her uncommon strength of character, and the ambition that had led her into politics in an age when career women were treated with either scorn or disbelief.

Cord wondered if her stubborn ambition could help him now.

"So Jennings is part of it?" she asked incredulously. "How do you think he fits in?"

"For starters, he's got the girl, Deborah Meyers. She found out something and they had to shut her up, so Jennings had her kidnapped—with the help of one of the tongs."

Melissa shook her head, as if to clear it. "You think that Jennings took her as . . . a slave, a captive?"

"Ask the On Leong. Slave girls are their specialty. Of course, if Jennings hadn't wanted her, they'd probably have killed her outright, so in a sense we owe him a favor."

"You ought to go thank him."

"I intend to—as soon as you've told me where to look for him."

"All right." Melissa wrote an address on the top sheet of her pad, tore it off, and handed it to Cord. "One thing you didn't explain: What happened to the globe you found in Kung Lin Saw's locker? Maybe I can get someone to analyze it for you."

"Good thinking." Cord reached under his shirt, and swore. From beneath it he pulled a handful of broken glass fragments, some stained greenish-gray. "It must have broken during the fight," he said. "Cut my back, but I didn't even know it at the time. Whatever that stuff was, it got all over me."

Melissa fingered one of the pieces. "There's writing on this one, Cord—two words in Chinese. Hop Lee"—she addressed the manservant—"tell us the meaning of these characters, please."

"Why, certainly, Miss Fallows." Hop Lee took the glass piece and bent to examine it. He was still looking when the silence was shattered with an animal growl, the same predatory roar they'd heard earlier.

"What *is* that thing?" McGee demanded.

Melissa smiled. "Don't worry, Captain. He's a pet."

"A pet? Mother of God! What kind of pet sounds like *that?*"

"I'll show you." The councilwoman stood up and led them to the back door of the clapboard house. Through it they could see a barren lot, stripped of all ground cover, facing the backs of other rundown houses. A leather leash was tied to a stake, planted in the ground. On the end of the leash was a full-grown mountain lion.

"I call him Mr. Scratch," said Melissa. "He's grouchy because it's nearly his feeding time."

Cord whistled. "He's grown a bit since I last saw him, hasn't he?"

Mr. Scratch strained at his leash, growling again. He was nearly nine feet long, and covered with fine, reddish-brown fur. Cord had first seen the puma when it was a cub, a fraction of its current size, mean-spirited even then—except toward Melissa. The months since then had done nothing to improve its disposition.

"I'll tell Hop Lee to feed him right away," said Melissa. "Poor thing."

"What's he eat?" asked McGee. "Careless neighbors?"

"Don't be silly, Captain. Mr. Scratch is as tame as you are—more so, I imagine." Boldly, she approached the animal, undaunted by its roaring. The big cat drew back into an attack crouch, poised as if to rip the life from her, but when Melissa extended her hand he hunched his neck and allowed himself to be scratched.

"Well, I'll be a dockwalloper," said McGee, taking a step forward. "To think that a monster like that could be tame as a kitten—"

Suddenly, the puma leaped forward, claws unsheathed, swiping at the captain's midsection. McGee could never have dodged fast enough, but before the cat could strike he hit the end of his leash and jerked backward, lashing at the air. Cord grabbed the shaken McGee and pulled him back, placating the animal.

"I probably should have warned you," said Melissa apologetically. "I can approach him; he doesn't mind that. But if anyone else does, he gets—shall we say— curious."

"Seems a damned sight more than curious to me," said McGee, massaging his neck.

Melissa gave the cat a final, reassuring stroke and rejoined the others. "I think he remembers you," she told Cord. "Remember how jealous he was, that time on the train . . . ?"

Cord nodded. "Why do you think I'm staying back here?"

"But I'm sure he'll be better after he's eaten. Bob Murchison gives me a good price on salted meats, shipped in from Sacramento."

"Tell me something," said Cord.

"What's that?"

"Why are you living out here? This is an odd place for a councilwoman, even if you didn't have a pet puma. Surely you can afford better."

Melissa smiled. "I'm living here precisely *because* I can afford better. Mayor Wylie lives in a house you could build ships in; Jake Jennings's mansion is even more extravagant. How are we supposed to represent the common people when we don't see them, don't talk to them, don't live like them? I think everyone on the city council should live like this."

"Preferably without the lions," said Cord.

Melissa led them back inside, and down the hall to the study. There they found Hop Lee, still examining the fragment of broken glass. His expression was unaccountably grim.

"What's the verdict, Lee?" asked Melissa, touching his shoulder. "Do you recognize the words?"

"I do," he said softly.

"What are they?"

Hop Lee glanced at Cord. "Mr. Diamondback, this was taken from a culture sample in a sealed glass dome?"

"That's right."

"And the globe shattered against your broken skin?"

"Yes."

"Then you are a dead man. The words on the glass are *incurable* and *fatal*." He lowered his eyes. "I'm sorry."

# 15

"It's a mistake," said Melissa Fallows, fiercely shaking her head. "I don't believe it, it's a mistake."

"No mistake," said Hop Lee, not raising his eyes.

"Well, it's a trick, then! They wanted Cord to think he'd been infected, so he'd give up the case, or—"

Cord shook his head. "Too farfetched, Melissa. They couldn't have known I'd be there, and take the globe, and break it against my skin. The message isn't a fake."

"So you believe it, then." Melissa looked at him with a stricken expression. "You think it's all over? You're going to give up?"

"I didn't say that." Cord tightened his gun belt. "Come on, McGee, we've got a girl to find."

"But you've got the plague, Cord! You're going to die! How can you act like nothing's wrong?"

Cord shrugged. For nearly seven years he'd been living on death's edge, constantly in danger from his violent past. Christopher Deacon's infamy had spread everywhere, and Cord had learned not to bank too heavily on the future.

But now that his death was certain—and probably quite soon—he felt an odd sense of relief, a freedom from the struggle to preserve his identity. In hours or days, a week at the most, it wouldn't matter if the entire United States knew that Chris Deacon and Cord Diamondback were the same. He could do what he liked, without having to cover his tracks.

And the first thing he planned to do was find Deborah Meyers, and empty his .44 into the body of her abductor.

"Let's go, McGee," Cord said. "I still want to pay a call on Jake Jennings."

"I'm coming," said the red-haired captain.

"So this is Nob Hill," said McGee. "I always wondered what this place was like. Looks even snootier than I expected."

"You're right about that," said Cord, as they guided their horses up the bountiful slope of California Street. Elegant mansions surrounded them, no two alike, a freewheeling riot of mismatched architectural styles. One was an exquisitely faced "gingerbread" pattern, four stories tall; beside it was the Crocker mansion, big and square and painted gloss white, like an oversized wedding cake.

"Jehosaphat!" said McGee, pointing at the Crocker mansion. "What the hell's that?"

Cord looked, too. A section was missing from the rear of the mansion, like a square bite out of the wedding cake; a three-sided, forty-foot partition cordoned off the mission section.

"That's the Spite Fence," Cord explained. "When Charles Crocker set out to build his house, he needed a big lot to put it in. He picked this one—but an undertaker named Yung already had a house on part of the property, and wouldn't sell it. So Crocker built his mansion *around* the guy's house, sealing it on three sides with that fence, to make it even more unliv-able."

"Nice fella," said McGee.

"Nice, rich fella," said Cord.

Beyond the Crocker mansion and the house with the gingerbread facing was another that dwarfed them both. It was incredibly tall, impossibly broad, and decorated in front with a double row of Corinthian columns under an overhang of white marble. The front door was framed by a twenty-foot stone arch, strewn with intricate carvings and surmounted by a gargoyle.

"The Jennings mansion," said Cord. "Jennings was the first of the silver millionaires. Story has it he came out here for the gold, missed the big strike, and got so mad he went out and found silver out of sheer stubbornness. Then he bought himself a seat on the city council, and he's been there ever since."

"So how do we get in?" asked McGee. "You want to sneak around back and look for an open window?"

"Oh, hell," said Cord, "let's break the door down."

"Hot damn!" McGee put his head down and took a running start at the sheet of paneled redwood. He smacked into it full force and bounced away, leaving a six-foot crack running lengthwise. He spat on his hands and snorted, stamping the ground, like a bull getting ready to charge. He rushed forward; the door splintered and broke away, spilling him into a carpeted foyer.

Cord kicked aside the remnants of the door and stepped in after him. A liveried servant rounded the corner just as McGee got to his feet; McGee grabbed the front of his uniform and pitched him out the doorway. Cord ran forward, scouting ahead.

Dining rooms opened on both sides of the hallway,

each with a different furniture style and dinner setting, all unused. Oil paintings in gilded frames hung at intervals along the wall. The paintings were portraits of stern-looking noblemen, finely dressed, with glistening hair and constipated features. At the end of the hall was a marble staircase, rising majestically to a second-story landing.

"See here! Who are you, sir?"

Cord spun to find an elderly manservant, dressed in his long johns, brandishing a single-shot musket. Cord grabbed the barrel of his weapon and pointed it at the ceiling. The servant pulled the trigger, but nothing happened.

"Old powder," said the servant dejectedly. "Knew I should have replaced it. Once it gets wet, you can't ever trust it afterward."

"Where's Jennings?" asked Cord.

The servant frowned, apparently considering his options. He looked at Cord, at the musket, at Cord again. He shrugged, said, "Upstairs, second right," and headed back to his bedroom.

"What was that about?" asked McGee, joining Cord at the foot of the stairs.

"Labor dispute," said Cord, starting up the stairs. He was halfway there when shots exploded from the upstairs landing, whanging off the balustrade at Cord's elbow. Cord ducked aside and pressed between the marble risers, drawing his gun. Above him, the gunman crouched behind a table, spraying the stairs with cartridges.

McGee made a dash up the stairs. The gunman swiveled to cover him, half-standing for a better shot. Cord fired twice, hitting him in the shoulder. The gunman spun away from the table, hit the rail at the edge of the landing, and pitched over it, catching his elbow between the rail supports. There was a brittle crunch as the man's elbow shattered, leaving him to dangle from his injured arm.

"Which of these doors has Jennings behind it?" yelled McGee. Cord reached the top of the stairs to find the captain breaking down the wrong door.

"It's this one," said Cord, rapping his knuckles on the second door from the left. He stood aside as both barrels of a shotgun blast tore a hole in the door at waist level. Cord reached through the hole, unlocked the door, and stepped through it to find Jake Jennings frantically reloading his shotgun.

"Where's the girl?" asked Cord, pointing his weapon at Jennings's belly.

The councilman looked up and turned pasty white. "She's safe," he insisted. "She's in a small cottage, not far from here."

"Where is it?" asked McGee, joining Cord at the door.

"I'll . . . I'll show you," said Jennings. He set his shotgun aside and crossed to a desk at the far wall, under a panoramic window. "I've got a map right here."

"That'd better be all you have," said Cord. "Carefully, now."

Jennings nodded, sifting through a clutter of ink-scrawled papers. "One thing I don't understand," he said timidly. "Why didn't Nightmare kill you, Diamondback? You've been a nuisance since you first arrived."

"That's the whole idea," said McGee, appearing in the doorway. "Him and me both, that is."

"You were looking for a map . . . ?" Cord reminded the councilman.

Jennings licked his silver mustache. "Ah, here it is."

"The map?"

"No, the plunger." He pulled a handle and a steel bar came up through a hole in the desktop. Beside the hole was a painted label reading COTTAGE. Jennings said, "What do you know about excavating, Diamondback?"

Cord frowned. "Why do you ask?"

"Because I've borrowed a trick from the forty-niners, used for blasting mines. It's a remote detonator, you see. This plunger is connected to a continuous wire, which runs from here to the cottage where the Meyers girl is staying. If I was to push this plunger—or if, say, you shot me and I fell on it—the girl you're seeking will be blown to fragments by twelve sticks of dynamite."

He grinned. "Drop your guns, please, both of you. And step back against that wall."

# 16

"Bullshit," said Cord.

"I mean it," said Jennings. "I don't want to kill her, but I will if I have to. Drop your guns, *now*. It's Deborah's only chance."

"Unless you're lying, that is."

"I'm not lying!" Jennings shoved some papers aside to reveal a full row of identical plungers, each with its own unique label. One said BOATHOUSE; another said COUNCIL CHAMBERS. "From this room I can obliterate a dozen locations, all over the city, with the press of a plunger. And each explosion will destroy the evidence of how it was caused! A self-concealing crime, you might say."

"What's the point?" asked Cord. "Why not just hire one of the Sydney Ducks to go over and set fire to it?"

"Because that would be too indirect," said Jennings. "I want control, complete control, right here in the palm of my hand." His fingers tightened on the plunger. "I despise embarrassment, Diamondback. Anything I find embarrassing—anywhere, throughout the city—is fitted with a dozen sticks of dynamite and a blasting cap on a wire. Watch, I'll show you."

Jennings took a different plunger in his free hand.

He raised it, braced himself, and slammed it down hard into the desktop. A sunburst of light appeared in the panoramic window behind him; moments later a rumbling tremor shook the room.

"One of my enemies," explained the councilman. "Or, rather, his house—and his family. Troublesome fellow, about time I dealt with him."

"Just like that?"

"Of course."

Cord hesitated, figuring his options. He could open fire, hoping Jennings would be thrown clear by the shots; or he could rush the man, trying to wrest him away from the plunger. Or he could simply turn around and leave. But all the choices had one thing in common: he'd be taking a terrible chance on Deborah's life.

Cord dropped his gun.

"What's the matter with you, Cord?" roared McGee. "Are you gonna let this son of a speckled prairie dog bitch get away with this?"

Cord shrugged. "I don't see how we have any choice."

"Well, *I've* got a choice! I'm going to perforate him if he doesn't let go of that damned plunger, right now."

"You're making a foolish mistake, Captain," said Jennings.

"I don't think—" McGee began, then broke off in mid-sentence as something hit the back of his neck. He gasped and crumpled to the floor. Behind him was a tall man with buck teeth and a switchback scar on his nose, holding a stout club.

"Works every time," the man said.

"Thank you, Ichabod," said Jennings, pulling a Derringer from the top desk drawer. "We'll deal with the captain momentarily, but first we'd better attend to Diamondback. He knows too much about this phylloxera thing."

"What do you want me to do?"

Jennings smiled benignly. "Kill him."

Ichabod pulled a tarnished Bowie knife from a sheath at his hip and started forward. "Where do you want it, mister?"

"Elsewhere," said Cord. He backed away, watching Ichabod's eyes, not his blade. When the other man tensed, ready to lunge, Cord waited a beat and sidestepped Ichabod's thrust. Cord grabbed an armful of linen from Jennings's bed and held it before him, slightly to one side, like a matador facing a bull.

"Hurry about it, would you?" said Jennings, glancing at his wall clock. "I've got other business to attend to."

"Why don't you just shoot him?" asked Ichabod. "You've got the gun."

"I'm above such things," sniffed Jennings.

Ichabod lunged again and Cord easily parried, using his linen shield to full advantage. Cord's reflexes were better than his opponent's, but it was only a stall; sooner or later he'd run out of dodging room in the enclosed space of the bedroom. Ichabod struck again and again, closer each time, and Cord found himself inevitably backed into a corner.

Then the knifeman swooped in, mean and fast, and tore a gash in the linen that missed Cord's thigh by a centimeter. Cord backed up, hit the wall, and realized he was trapped. His options were exhausted, his escape blocked off, his death inevitable.

But wasn't he already a walking dead man?

With nothing to lose, Cord bunched the linen in front of him and sprang forward, taking the other man by surprise. Ichabod paused for only an instant, then swung his knife around. Cord felt the blade hit his rib cage and glance off into the bedding; he caught Ichabod's hand and twisted hard, breaking the wrist. Ichabod screamed and stumbled backward into Jennings's desk. The knife clattered to the floor.

"You fool," said Jennings. "Listen, Diamondback, be still or I'll kill the girl. Now, Ichabod, once again—kill him."

"But he broke my wrist!" said Ichabod, cradling it against his side.

"You've got another one," said Jennings.

Cord noticed something: Jennings's desk had slid away from the wall when Ichabod smashed into it. Behind it was a cluster of wires, loosely bound together, disappearing into a mousehole at the base of the wall. The desk was perhaps six feet from where he was standing.

"I can't kill him with a broken wrist," Ichabod whined. "I need help, I need a doctor—"

"Oh, for Christ's sake," said Jennings. He sighed, raised his Derringer, and opened fire on Diamondback. Cord dove aside, snatched up Ichabod's knife, and rolled behind the desk, grasping the bundled wires. With one slice he severed them.

"What the hell—" Jennings slammed down the plunger and turned pale when nothing happened. He raised and lowered it again and again, feverishly, glancing fretfully out the window at the undisturbed city.

"Ichabod," he said, backing away, "go to the cottage and kill the girl. Diamondback, you're a dead man."

Cord said nothing.

Jennings moved around the desk, poised to fire,

holding his gun in both hands. Cord stood up and threw the knife, hitting the councilman in the right eye. Jennings fired reflexively, putting two slugs in the wall and grazing Cord's neck with a third. Then he fell backward against his bed, dropping the Derringer.

Cord looked around. Ichabod was gone. And Deborah was dead if no one stopped him.

"One last job," said Jennings weakly. "Just one."

Cord looked over to see what he was talking about. Jennings fumbled under his bed, pulled out a detonator, and raised its plunger. "Good-bye—"

Cord dove through the panoramic window as the world came apart behind him.

# 17

It took years for Cord to hit the ground.

He seemed to hang suspended, dropping like a marble through molasses as debris spun off around him, spouting tongues of flame. Cord couldn't hear anything, but it wasn't silence; it was the opposite of silence—pure, white noise, like a thunderclap that wouldn't fade.

Then something hit him, hard. And fingernails tore at his face. And he bounced and rolled and smacked into something so hard and big it could only be the ground, and it was soft but not soft enough. Cord felt unconsciousness descending and he really didn't care to fight it off.

Until he remembered that Deborah Meyers was going to die.

He groaned, sat up, groaned again. He was lying next to a topiary hedge, in a courtyard in back of the Jennings mansion. The hedge had been cut and shaped to resemble an elephant, but it looked like its back was broken—from the impact of Cord's fall. Cord realized that this botanical ornament had probably saved his life.

He stood up, feeling the strain in his legs, arms, and shoulders. Nothing was broken; he could walk well enough, if he didn't walk fast, but he wasn't up to much else. A slurpy roar seemed to fill his ears as his hearing wavered in and out again.

Cord starting walking. Carefully, he worked his way back to the street, keeping to the shadows and staying well clear of the gathering crowd. The Jennings's mansion was already a total loss, engulfed in flames, reduced in minutes from an architectural masterpiece to a sprawling ruin. The councilman had known exactly where to place his charges.

Cord wondered if Ichabod might have been caught in the explosion, like Jennings's other men—and, he suddenly realized, Beefeater McGee. The red-bearded captain had surely been incinerated at the moment of detonation; not even McGee's steel-studded hide could withstand an inferno like this one. Cord felt a sudden, stinging sense of loss.

But grief was for another time. Cord put it aside, scanning the crowd of morbid sightseers for any sign of Ichabod. Most were casually dressed: a plump man and his wife wore flannel long johns and slippers, and a serious-looking citizen beside them was frantically buckling his suspenders. Close behind was a yawning woman with frowzy hair, and a tall man with buck teeth and a switchback scar on his nose.

The man with the scar was loping down the street. Cord fell in behind him.

Ichabod was heading north, in a hurry. Cord struggled to keep the pace without being seen. He still felt groggy, and his legs wobbled with every step, but it helped to breathe the cool night air and concentrate on his goal. It couldn't be *too* far, Cord reasoned, if Jennings had rigged it with a continuous wire from his bedroom.

Ichabod turned into a sidestreet and ducked into an

alley between two gray-bricked buildings. Cord waited a few moments and followed him, afraid the scarred killer would turn and see him, but desperate not to fall behind. Cord entered the alley as Ichabod was leaving it; the tall man was still in sight when Cord emerged onto a muddy street, sloping toward the bay.

Cord began to wonder if they would ever get to Deborah's makeshift prison. Already it seemed he'd been walking for most of his adult life, and the tall man showed no signs of slowing down. Worse, Ichabod was widening the distance between them, and Cord was too weak and dizzy to close the gap.

I'll have to kill him, Cord thought grimly, as his consciousness began to fade. I'll shoot him and find Deborah later, after I've had a nice nap. He groped for his gun, couldn't find it, and realized with horror that he'd left it in the wreckage of Jennings's mansion.

Up ahead, Ichabod turned a corner and vanished from sight. Cord hurried after him and nearly sprawled flat as a rock rolled under his foot. He steadied himself, fighting back nausea, ignoring the hammer blows that burst in his skull with every step. Stopping wasn't an option: if Ichabod escaped him, Victoria would never see her daughter again.

Cord reached the corner and looked wildly around. The street was nearly deserted, half lit in the glow of windows and streetlamps. A cat licked itself in the front seat of a buckboard parked alongside the road.

Ichabod was no longer walking.

He stood before a small, unpainted waterfront cottage, fumbling in his pocket for a key ring. After a moment he got the door open, stepped inside, and pulled it shut behind him.

Cord ran for the door. He tripped and fell on his

face. He got up, rubbed his neck, kept going. He reached the door and found it locked. Inside, someone screamed.

Cord shambled along the side of the cottage, looking for a way in. Along the side wall was another door, also locked, and a boarded-up window. Neither would budge when Cord pressed against them. But in the back was an unbroken window, set at waist height, and through it Cord could see Deborah Meyers.

She was stripped to the waist, and tied by the wrists to a hook set in the ceiling. Welts and bruises covered her shoulders, and a burn scar crossed both breasts. Ichabod held a straight razor in his left hand; he was tormenting her, inflicting minor cuts on her breasts and stomach, touching the blade to her throat. Deborah squirmed away, wrenching at her bonds, as Ichabod prodded her nipple with the blade.

Cord felt a rush of wild rage, an adrenaline surge that obliterated his fatigue. He backed up, ran three steps, and smashed through the window, somersaulting onto the floor of the cottage.

He looked up to find Ichabod right on top of him. The tall man slashed down with his razor, laying open Cord's cheek. Cord swung his leg up, caught Ichabod across the neck, and kicked him backward into a table. Ichabod howled in pain, favoring his broken wrist—but his left hand still held the razor.

Cord tore a strip from his shirt and held it to his face, trying to staunch the bleeding. Ichabod moved in cautiously, twirling the razor in little circles. Lamplight gleamed off the point of the blade. Deborah watched intently.

Ichabod feinted left, struck right. Cord ducked aside and kicked at Ichabod's groin. Ichabod grunted and fell back, doubling over. Cord grabbed a wooden chair and smashed it over Ichabod's head. Ichabod swayed like a sapling, almost fell, lunged suddenly, and sliced open the side of Cord's shirt.

Cord stepped back, putting some distance between them. Ichabod crouched low, his razor poised for a fatal slash. Neither moved. Sea gulls shrieked in the distance.

Dizziness washed over Cord. He blinked, feeling the curling edge of oblivion pressing in on his temples. The room seemed to tilt under him, and the roar of the ocean filled his ears. He almost didn't notice when Ichabod rushed in and buried his razor in Cord's forearm.

It hurt like hell, but the pain was someone else's, not his. Cord saw the fight from a great distance, like a theater play seen from the balcony. He was wounded, bleeding, semiconscious—but he couldn't let go until Deborah was safe. She needed him, needed him badly.

Cord reached through the fog, found Ichabod's broken wrist, and gave it a quarter turn. Ichabod screamed and toppled to the floor. Cord looked around for the razor, then remembered it was stuck in his arm. He pulled it free and sliced Ichabod's throat with it. Ichabod grabbed his neck as blood spurted between his fingers.

Cord's vision winked out, came back again. He looked up to find Deborah, still tied to the ceiling hook, watching him with horrified fascination. He took the razor and carefully cut her bonds. Deborah slumped against the wall, breathing deeply, rubbing her wrists where the rope had chafed them.

Cord dropped the razor and sat down heavily on the floor.

"Are you . . . are you one of them?" asked

Deborah. She took a tentative step forward, covering her breasts with one arm. "Are you—"

"I'm Diamondback," said Cord. "I came to take you home."

"Oh, thank God! I thought you were—"

Deborah stopped. She gaped at him in stark, slack-jawed horror; Cord realized that his shirt was hanging open, exposing his scars. He opened his mouth to explain and Deborah hit him with a chair leg on the side of the head. He sank to the floor and lost track of everything.

Deborah Meyers ran through the darkened streets of San Francisco, trying to stay out of sight, hugging herself against the chill. The fog was beginning to roll in from the bay, dampening the city with a cold, cloying mist, and Deborah wished she had the cotton blouse that Jennings had stripped from her when she'd been abducted in Chinatown.

She had to keep running, had to find help. Councilman Jennings was part of a conspiracy, a plan that threatened the entire city. Others were in on it, too. But worst of all was what she'd just discovered: at the heart of the scheme was Christopher Deacon, brutal murderer of Billy Fallows.

She'd get help, tell them about Deacon. She'd describe him, and the scars, and say he went by the name of Diamondback. And they'd track him down like the dog he was and hang the bastard by daybreak.

She hoped his neck wouldn't break. It would be so much better if he strangled to death, slowly.

# 18

"Wake up, range rat," said Beefeater McGee.

Cord blinked in astonishment and stared up at the red-haired face. "McGee? What are you—"

"Trying to keep you alive, is what I'm doing," said McGee. "You should see yourself, Cord. Your body looks like a trail map of Colorado. Is there any place you're not cut, bruised, or bleeding?"

"Big toe," said Cord, trying to sit up. The room wobbled around him, like a wagon with a bad wheel, and spots darted in and out of his vision. Cord rubbed his neck, wincing at the bullet wound from Jennings's revolver. He frowned and said, "Hold on, McGee. Why aren't you dead? When that house blew up—"

"I was halfway out of it, following Ichabod. I figured he'd lead me to the girl, but I lost him in the explosion. Good thing you were backing me up, Cord." McGee looked at the wrecked furniture and Ichabod's body, sprawled in the center of a dried blood-puddle. "By the time I found you fellas, it was all over."

"What about the girl?" Cord asked anxiously. "Where is she?"

"Beats me." McGee shrugged his gigantic shoulders.

"Don't worry, Cord, she must've run off in a panic. She'll turn up soon enough."

"I hope so." Cord tried to stand up, but his legs gave out from under him. McGee caught him and lowered him to the floor.

"Easy, Cord, you've got a concussion. Could be you were a little too close to the dynamite when it went off."

"It's possible," Cord admitted.

"Yeah, well, it'll pass in a few minutes—but you're not going to fight any more maniacs this evening."

"Vicky," said Cord. "I've got to tell Vicky what happened." He tried to stand up again, but the slurpy roar came back, and the room teetered and spun out of reach, and he knew he was falling but it took forever to hit the floor . . .

Cord woke up only once on the back of McGee's horse. He was bobbing in and out of consciousness, and couldn't be sure of anything he saw or heard. But he seemed to hear something far away, hoarse shouts and scattered gunfire, and the sound of a woman screaming. And heat, fearsome heat, washing over him in scalding waves. And smoke, and a smell like roast pork, and the distant boom of an explosion.

Then it passed, and Cord felt nothing.

"Mother of God!" Melissa Fallows was saying. "What happened to him?"

"He had a run-in with one of Jennings's men," said McGee. "The other guy's worse off, believe me. Where should I put him?"

"On the sofa. Hop Lee"—her voice was muffled as she turned aside—"get me some bandages and a basin of hot water. And some of that medical cream, right away."

"Certainly, Miss Fallows." Footsteps receded into the hallway, and Cord felt himself lowered onto soft cushions. From down the hall came the sound of running water.

Cord opened his eyes. Melissa was watching him with obvious concern, and McGee hovered in the background. Droplets of blood soiled the carpet.

"Sorry to put you to all this trouble," he said.

"Cord, you're alive! And awake," said Melissa. "I was beginning to wonder."

"Not me," said McGee. "I figured he'd be up and around after a quick forty winks. How you feeling, buddy?"

"Like a dead mule." Cord sat up on the couch, as Hop Lee returned with a basin and an armful of supplies. Cord was stiff and sore—a feeling he knew very well—and dizzy, if he moved too fast. But what puzzled him was that his shirt didn't fit, and seemed much too small for him.

"Don't worry none about the shirt," said McGee, sensing his confusion. "Yours was all bloody and torn up, so I swapped it with that kidnapper fella's, the one you were fighting. I don't reckon he'll miss it none."

Cord relaxed, grateful for McGee's foresight. If Melissa had seen his scars, as Deborah had, his problems would be compounded. But Deborah was still out there, confused and panicked, and Cord couldn't predict what she'd do. In a few minutes it might not matter if Melissa knew his secret or not.

"Hold still, now." Melissa moistened a cloth pad and gingerly touched his cheek with it. Cord flinched as Melissa dressed the wound. "Nasty cut you've got here," she said. "Not deep, but you ought to have stitches in it. The arm, too."

"Some other time," said Cord. "I have things to

do." He smiled, wincing as the skin of his cheek pulled tight. "Besides, I've got a few spots left uninjured."

"For a while, at least. Hold still." Melissa wrapped a bandage around his forearm, binding it tightly, knotting the ends together. "McGee says you found the girl, then lost her again."

"That's right. Any sign of her since?"

"No, nothing." Melissa shrugged. "What's your next move?"

"I don't know. I'll have to think about it." He cocked his head as a distant, rumbling roar sounded somewhere outside. "What was that?"

"The Vigilance Committee. They went berserk when they found out about the plague. Now they're tearing up the whole town, looking for plague spots they can set fire to. Trouble is, some of the property owners don't like seeing their land destroyed." She sighed. "So far there are five deaths, sixteen injuries, incalculable property damage. The mayor is considering declaring a crisis."

"But what started the plague scare? I thought the council was keeping it under wraps."

"So did I," said Melissa. "But it turns out . . . well, show him, McGee."

McGee pulled a newspaper from the living room table and showed it to Cord. It was a special late edition of the *San Francisco Examiner*, and it featured a banner headline:

PLAGUE COMES IN ON DEATH SHIP,
THOUSANDS EXPECTED TO DIE.

Cord took the newspaper and scanned the headline story. The first paragraph described how the *Orpheus* had entered the harbor with all its crew dead, apparently victims of plague. A doctor sent to investigate had not returned alive. Others were thought to be already infected. The mayor could not be reached for comment.

The article quoted several inflammatory remarks from City Councilman Heywood Mars.

"So much for secrecy," said Cord, casting the paper aside. "How does Mars defend his decision to go public with it? Didn't he realize the consequences?"

"Nobody knows," said Melissa. "Heywood dropped out of sight shortly after the paper came out. Do you think he's tied up in it somehow?"

"Yes. I just hope we can stop him before the city goes up in flames."

"Speaking of which," said McGee, "I've got a ship in the harbor, and the vigilantes aren't too charitable toward visitors from out of town. Take care of Diamondback here, Miss Fallows. I've got a boat to defend."

McGee spun on his heel and barreled out the door. Hop Lee ducked aside to keep from colliding with the departing captain.

"You can go, too, Lee," said Melissa, finishing up with Cord's injuries. "I think Cord needs a different kind of therapy now."

"Very well, Miss Fallows," said Hop Lee, bowing silently as he closed the door behind him.

# 19

"It's been a while, hasn't it?" said Melissa, sitting beside him. "Mr. Scratch was just a cub when I met you on that train."

"He hasn't gotten any less ferocious since then," said Cord.

"Neither have I," said Melissa.

She was wearing an amber dress, tied at the hip with a wide sash. She tugged the sash and it pulled free, whispering over the satiny fabric. Cord felt himself responding as Melissa stretched her arms above her head, framing her buttery-colored blond hair, pressing her breasts against the smooth cloth.

"I'd better check you for injuries . . . elsewhere," she said.

Melissa leaned forward and undid his pants, not hurrying, watching Cord steadily. Cord liked the suppressed savagery in Melissa's eyes, a primal hunger that was never quite appeased—like a tigress in heat, he thought, as she slid her hand over the swelling in his groin.

"Seems healthy enough," said Melissa, with mock seriousness. "But I'd better make"—her left eyebrow rose—"a more thorough examination."

"Can't be too careful," Cord agreed.

Melissa pulled his boots off, then his socks—and she bent to lick the instep of his left foot with a slow, luxuriant stroke of her tongue. "It's an Oriental custom," she said, "to make a man feel more . . . agreeable." She sat up, reached for his pants, and worked them down over Cord's legs.

"Now the shirt," she said, starting to unbutton it.

Cord shook his head, wincing. "I'd rather you didn't, Melissa. My arm's still tender. I don't want to irritate the wound."

"Well . . . all right." Melissa slid her finger along Cord's legs, starting with his ankles, on to his knees and across his thighs, teasingly tickling his leg hairs. She stopped just short of his rail-straight penis, and returned to his feet—not stroking, but licking, moistening, kissing her way up the tan roughness of his skin.

Cord felt the pain of his other injuries recede to a dull, background haze, all but lost in the riptide of eroticism. Melissa worked her way across his thighs, leaving a moist trail over his skin, always stopping tauntingly close to Cord's penis without ever quite touching it. With a teasing chuckle she moved away, sliding outward toward his hips. She kissed him there, too, and held his buttocks with both hands, pulling him upward toward her.

She kissed his penis.

Not a long, sloppy kiss, but the briefest touch of her lips on his flesh—enough to kindle a blaze of feeling, then quench it just as abruptly with her tantalizing withdrawal. She laughed, then bent to kiss him again just as briefly. Then she ran her tongue along the full length of his shaft, and back again, a tactile tour that seemed to last forever. Cord felt the pressure building inside him, like storm currents pounding at weakening floodgates.

"Roll over," said Melissa.

"Now?"

"Right now." She helped him roll onto his stomach, careful of his injured arm. She kneaded the hard muscles of his calves and thighs, pressing, stretching, bearing down and releasing again. Cord felt a wave of relaxation wash over him, like the warm waters of a mineral bath. Melissa worked her way upward, massaging his back and shoulders.

"Is your back hurt, too?" she asked abruptly. "Feels like scars, or something."

"It's a burn," said Cord. "From a long time ago. No need to worry about it now."

"Well, maybe I should have a look at it anyway."

"I'd rather you kept massaging."

"All right." She resumed kneading his back, more gently than before. Then she moved to his neck, squeezing the muscular folds between her fingers, ducking down to kiss him behind the ear. Cord sighed as the tension dropped away from him.

"Roll over again," said Melissa.

He did. Melissa stood up, grasped the hem of her amber dress in both hands, and pulled it gracefully over her head. She wore nothing underneath. Her body was as perfect as Cord remembered, clean and soft and brown as a polished wood carving, glistening in a fine envelope of perspiration.

She stood for a moment, admiring him as he admired her. Then she crouched by the side of the sofa and took his penis fully into her mouth, moving her lips back and forth, stroking his balls with a manicured fingernail. Just as Cord could stand it no longer she pulled free, straddled him, and lowered herself slowly and sensually onto his penis.

Cord strained upward to meet her. She pushed him down again, then rode with his next thrust, holding him tightly between her legs as he bucked furiously up and down. Melissa made a strangled, moaning sound, from way down in her throat, and Cord felt her shuddering with urgency as the climax overtook her. He waited for her to finish, then thrust into her even more fiercely.

Melissa gasped as she realized Cord was still pumping. She felt herself caught in the grip of his arousal, impaled on Cord as he thrashed under her in a pleasurable frenzy. Melissa thought wildly of Mr. Scratch, straining at his leash, a creature of raw, bestial impulse, beyond polite human affairs.

Cord exploded inside her. Melissa felt a second orgasm coming on, obliterating all reason. She reeled, toppled forward on Cord, spent of her energy by their mutual release. Cord held her firmly against the padded velvet of the sofa cushions.

"You're getting better with age, Cord," she said.

"Could be," Cord admitted. "In another fifty years I should be just about perfect."

She chuckled. "I doubt it'll take that long."

"Thirty, then."

"Nope. You're fine right now." She stretched her arms over her head, pressing her breasts against Cord's rib cage. "At least, as far as I can tell."

"So you're an expert?"

"I'm a woman."

"I noticed." Cord touched his fingers to her lips, and she kissed them one by one. She looked up at him.

"I'll bet this is the most fun you've had with a member of the city council," she said.

"You've got me there," Cord admitted. "The others don't do a thing for me. But what happened to the senate race? Are you still determined to follow in your father's footsteps?"

"Determined as never before. My father was a bastard, Cord, but that doesn't hold up for the rest of the family. I'm going to make up for him, and then some. Next year I'll start campaigning for the senatorial elections."

"Think you'll pull it off?"

"Well, it's still not easy. If women could vote, I'd stand a better chance. This country's laws are still medieval, in some ways—but a woman senator's not impossible. I got on the city council, didn't I?"

"You sure did."

"I won't deny my father's reputation played a part—deserved or otherwise. But once I'm in office it won't matter how I got there. I'm going a write a whole new chapter in this state's history."

"You might, at that." Cord was about to make another observation when the silence was broken by the sound of rapid footsteps, and four sharp knocks on the living room door.

"Miss Fallows?" asked the voice of her servant.

"Yes, Lee, what is it?"

"Councilman Heywood Mars is at the door, demanding to see you. He says it's important, something that could affect the whole city. Do you want me to let him in?"

# 20

Heywood Mars looked even paler than usual. He brushed past Hop Lee as soon as the servant let him into the living room, and he lowered his stout frame into a chair.

"We're in trouble, Melissa," he said, mopping his brow with an embroidered handkerchief. "I don't know what's all going to come of all this."

"Never mind," said Melissa fiercely, snatching the *Chronicle*'s special edition from a side table. "What's the meaning of releasing this story? Do you have any idea of the panic this is going to cause?"

A distant, muffled crash punctuated her words.

Mars glanced fearfully at the article, and back again at Melissa. "I didn't mean—that is, they distorted my words. They exaggerated. I issued a carefully worded advisory to this paper, explaining the danger of plague and asking all citizens to stay calm. But by the time Hearst's boys got through with it"—he sneered at the paper—"they turned it into the end of the goddamned world! I never meant to cause any trouble!"

"I believe you, but it doesn't help us now. Why did you go to the papers in the first place? I thought we agreed not to."

Mars licked his fat, watery lips. "I had to, Melissa.

The people had to be warned. Every day we kept quiet risked hundreds—thousands—of lives. I couldn't keep quiet about a plague outbreak forever!"

Melissa glanced at Cord. Cord rubbed his chin and said, "How do you know that it *is* plague? Carpenter never made his report, and my work is unfinished. Aren't you jumping to conclusions?"

"No. I brought in an expert to examine one of the plague victims. Thirty minutes ago he made a positive diagnosis. Primary pneumonic plague, the deadliest disease known to man."

Hop Lee made a gasping sound and edged away from Diamondback. Melissa glanced at him uneasily, and at the glass shard on the table with its terrible inscription: INCURABLE and FATAL. Heywood Mars turned his handkerchief inside out, looking for a dry spot to mop his forehead.

"One question," said Diamondback.

Mars's head bobbed up. "Uh . . . yes?"

"Who was the victim your expert examined? Rheingold and his friend were cremated. Of course, there were other bodies on the plague ship, but I didn't see any lines forming to go over there and get one."

"It wasn't necessary," said Mars. "We found another victim, not far from the waterfront. Worst case I've seen yet. Poor girl never had a chance."

Melissa's hand tightened on the arm of the sofa. "My God, Heywood! Who?"

"Same girl Diamondback's looking for. Deborah Meyers."

Melissa looked stricken. Mars wrung his hands in his handkerchief. Hop Lee shifted from one foot to the other, looking thoroughly uncomfortable.

"So where do you stand in all of this?" asked Cord. "Do you stand to lose much in the rioting?"

"Probably not," said Mars. "I don't own much land. Most of my money's in shipping, and the freighters are out at sea. But the merchants I deal with could be wiped out in the rioting, and that could affect my business, too."

"Sure could," Cord observed. "Especially if you were overstocked on supplies—say, in those freighters you mentioned—so you could move in after the crisis and get business started again. For a fee." Cord steepled his fingers. "How much do you figure to make off this epidemic, Mars?"

Heywood Mars purpled. "Why, that's preposterous! How can you suggest such a thing, that I would endanger thousands of lives—"

"You've already endangered one," said Cord. "When you and Jennings had Deborah Meyers kidnapped, she was in real trouble for a while—at least, until I broke in and set her loose."

"You found her? But how—"

"I found her and lost her again. That was maybe two hours ago. But I had a real good look at her then—she wasn't wearing much—and I didn't see any of the plague symptoms that Dr. Carpenter told us to look for. Not only that, but she seemed in excellent health, especially considering the ordeal she'd just been through."

Cord smiled grimly. "From the first onset of the plague, it's at least a full day until the victim dies. But you'd have her dead in less than two hours, even if she got sick right after I saw her. No sale, Mars. Jennings had a partner, and I'm betting it's you."

"A partner?" said Melissa. "You never told us that."

Cord's eyes never left Mars. "It's true. Nightmare mentioned someone called 'the Master,' Jennings's superior. The Master has been pulling the strings since this thing started, and who better than the owner of the ship that brought the plague?

"Mars wanted to raise the value of his goods, and he didn't care how he did it. So he got a plague culture somewhere—how, I don't know—and had it brought here on the *Orpheus*. But it got loose and killed the crew. The whole plan would have collapsed if Fergus Rheingold hadn't brought the plague in on his life raft."

"But he did," said Melissa. "And now both you and Deborah are infected. I'm so sorry, Cord."

"Don't be. I'll go when the times comes, but Deborah wasn't infected. She was kidnapped first, before she ever got to Rheingold. Isn't that true, Mars?"

"Of course not," said the councilman. "This is the most damnable pack of lies I've ever heard, and if you support this wild accusation, Melissa"—he stuck his finger at her—"I'll have you bounced out of your council seat before you can say two syllables in public."

"How many sites of infection were there?" Cord demanded. "How far do we need to post a quarantine?"

Mars leaped to his feet, sputtering with anger. "I won't be insulted like this, not another minute! I'm leaving!"

"Sit down," said Cord.

Mars bolted for the door. Cord caught up with him, grabbed his collar, and slammed his head into the wall. Mars stumbled backward, swearing profusely, punching at the air. Cord sent a left hook into his nose that dropped him onto the carpet, bleeding.

"Perhaps the Vigilance Committee should hear

about this," said Melissa. "They'll probably put a rope around his neck, and I can't say I blame them. When I think of him sitting on the council—"

"You've got the wrong man," said a voice from the doorway.

Cord turned and felt a shock run through his body. Standing in the doorway was Deborah Meyers, wearing a poorly fitting buckskin coat, pointing a Smith and Wesson .44-.40 right at him.

"He's the man behind it, Miss Fallows," said Deborah, keeping her gun on Cord. "He's Christopher Deacon, the man who killed your father. He's got the same scars on his back. And I say we kill him, right now."

# 21

"Take it easy, Deborah," said Melissa, getting up to comfort her. "You've been through a terrible shock, and you're—"

"No! I saw the scars; I didn't imagine them. Tell him to take his shirt off if you don't believe me. He's Christopher Deacon, and he should pay for what he's done."

"But he *can't* be Deacon," Melissa insisted. "I've known him for almost two years. He tried to help Uncle Dale, when those bandits attacked us. Don't you think I would have found out if he were my father's killer?"

Deborah Meyers was unmoved—a trait, Cord realized, that she shared with her mother. How many times had Victoria won a case by stubbornly sticking to the evidence, against a wealth of testimony? Cord admired her persistence, even under the circumstances.

"Think back, Miss Fallows," said Deborah, holding tight to the .44-.40. "Hasn't he ever done anything odd, anything you couldn't explain? There must have been something."

"Don't be silly," Melissa began, then hesitated, eyes narrowed.

"What is it, Miss Fallows?"

"Well . . . Cord and I . . . we were intimate, a short while ago, and . . . he wouldn't take off his shirt." She frowned, remembering. "And on the train, two years ago . . . he didn't take it off then, either." She turned to face Cord, eyes widening in astonishment. "Is it true? Are you Christopher Deacon?"

Cord hesitated. This was the moment he'd been dreading: the exposure, in front of witnesses, of his deadliest secret. He knew what could happen if he told the truth, but Deborah had the gun—and the scars on his back were proof positive of her claims. Only by admitting everything could he hope to win their silence.

Of course, Heywood Mars would never be persuaded—but he was out cold on the floor.

"It's true," said Cord.

The color drained from Melissa's face.

"I killed Billy Fallows," he went on, "because he murdered my brother and would have gone unpunished. He wasn't a saint, Melissa. You told me so yourself. He was a fiend, overdue for killing, and I don't regret being his executioner."

Melissa fell silent, too stunned to make any comment. But Deborah spoke up, and there was little doubt about *her* feelings.

"Horseshit, you bastard! I met Billy Fallows once, at a church picnic. He was the sweetest, purest man who ever lived. He told me I could work for him when I got out of school. How can you say those things?"

"Did you know he was a white slaver?" Cord asked coldly. "A lot of girls like you *did* work for him, turning ten tricks a night in one of his Barbary Coast brothels. Did he mention that at your church picnic?"

"You're lying," said Deborah. Tears formed in her eyes, but she fought them back, holding the gun steady. "You'd say anything to save your filthy hide."

"He smuggled narcotics, too. But he didn't just sell to the addicts. He'd kidnap innocent people, get them addicted with regular injections, then turn them loose—as clients. One of his forced customers was twelve years old."

"How—how could you know all this?" asked Deborah. "Even if it *was* true, how could you know it?"

"My brother dug it up. He spent all his time on the Fallows case, and he got more than he bargained for. But the senator didn't like having his dirty underwear exposed. That's why he killed Eric, and that's why I killed him."

For a moment there was absolute silence. Cord's words hung in the air, like a sharp, unpleasant smell. Deborah looked puzzled, but Cord knew she was unconvinced.

Melissa Fallows cleared her throat. "I think . . . he's telling the truth," she said. She looked at Cord in astonishment, like someone waking from a dream. "It fits; it all makes sense. Deborah, he's right about my father—every word. They should give Cord a medal for killing the bastard. I wanted to do it myself."

Melissa reached for the gun, but Deborah backed away, still covering Cord. "No!" she cried. "I don't believe it! It's all lies! Why would so many people hate you if you didn't do anything wrong?"

"Because they don't know what happened," said Cord. "And they don't care, so long as they've got a scapegoat. But one person does know, Deborah. She knows everything."

"Who?"

"Your mother. Victoria knew right from the start; she helped me get away and make a new life for myself. She wanted Billy Fallows dead as much as I did, maybe more. You see, Deborah"—Cord picked his words carefully—"your mother loved Eric Deacon. For a while they were planning to get married. But Eric was trying to start up his law practice, and your mother was working her way through school, and there wasn't time to raise a family.

"Then Victoria got pregnant, and it changed everything. Eric wanted to marry her then, but Victoria refused. She said it would ruin his reputation—and his career—to father a child conceived out of wedlock. And nothing Eric said would change her mind."

Deborah looked thunderstruck. "Are you saying that Eric Deacon was my father? And Billy Fallows killed him?"

Cord nodded.

"But . . . how do I know I can believe you? What if you're just making all this up?"

"You know I'm not," said Cord. "It fits too well. But one last thing: Victoria wears a locket around her neck, all the time. You must have seen it, must have guessed it was a gift from your father. Have you ever noticed the inscribed initials?"

"ED," Deborah whispered. Her gun wavered; she sighed, and pointed it at the floor. "I never knew who my father was," she said softly. "Mom always said it was best I didn't know. I never understood her, till now." She shook her head. "I'm sorry, Christopher— *Uncle* Christopher. I didn't know, didn't realize . . ."

"You couldn't have known," said Cord.

"You were trying to save me, weren't you? At the cottage, I mean."

Cord nodded. "But I got more than I bargained for. That was quite a clout you gave me, young lady." He touched a sore spot on his temple.

"Oh, Christopher—"

"Cord, if you don't mind. Just for appearances." He glanced meaningfully at Melissa, who smiled and nodded back.

"Oh, Cord, when I think of how close I came to killing you—well, I found this gun in a looted store and I went a little crazy, I guess. But I'm sorry now. I swear I'll never tell a soul about who you are and what you did . . ."

She started forward to embrace him. She was smiling broadly when Heywood Mars came to life and grabbed her gun and pressed its barrel into Deborah's throat, pinning her arms behind her.

"Very touching," said Mars, pulling Deborah with him toward the doorway. "And very informative, too. I'm sure I can make good use of Christopher Deacon's reward money, in addition to my other profits. Please don't move, Deacon, while I'm shooting you—or I'll blast this little girl's brains all over the ceiling."

Laughing, he took aim and opened fire.

# 22

Mars fired twice at point-blank range. Both shots missed, because Deborah wrapped herself around Mars's gun hand and flung herself sideways. Angrily, Mars pulled free, but Cord used the extra seconds to lunge forward and grab Mars's gun and force it back until the barrel was pointed at Mars's nose.

"Try it now," Cord suggested.

Panicked, Mars let go of the gun. Cord said, "Thank you," shifted his grip, and pistol-whipped Mars three times, raising vicious welts on his soft face. Cord tossed the gun aside and threw an old-fashioned haymaker at Mars's jaw. The councilman hit the wall and bounced face down onto the carpet.

"That's enough, Cord," said Melissa. "You don't want to kill him."

"Don't I?" Cord sighed. "Well, maybe not right away. Let's find out what he knows, at least."

"Couldn't hurt."

Cord grabbed Mars's shoulder and rolled him onto his back. He was stooping to lift the councilman when Mars opened his eyes and said, "You're finished, bastard." He raised his fist, pointed it at Cord, and squeezed. Something went *bang!* and a bullet parted Cord's hair.

Cord rolled aside as another shot hit the ceiling. Mars scrambed to his feet, making a break for the door, but Hop Lee got in his way. Mars raised his fist and squeezed twice more; Hop Lee collapsed against the doorjamb, clutching his shoulder.

Mars stumbled past him, pausing on the threshold for a parting shot at Cord. Cord snatched up Deborah's .44-.40 and shot a chunk out of Mars's neck with it. Mars screamed and blundered down the hallway.

"Be careful, Cord," said Melissa, as Cord sprinted after him. "He's got a squeezer, and there's three shots left."

"I know," said Cord. He dove into the hallway, ready to shoot back if Mars was waiting in ambush with his trick weapon. But Mars probably felt out-matched against a revolver; his palm-held squeezer was made for surprise, not firepower, and it had no accuracy except at close range. Cord brought up the .44-.40, sighting down the hallway, but Mars was gone.

Footsteps sounded behind him.

Cord whirled, tracking with his revolver. Mars had fled the wrong way in his panic; he was running away from the door, farther into the house. Cord fired just as Mars ducked around the corner, by the study. Spat-tered blood marked his path over the carpet.

Cord lit out after him. He reached the corner in six big strides, raised his gun, and fired at Mars's retreating back as the councilman stumbled out the back door. Mars jerked under the impact of Cord's bullet but kept running, just as Melissa yelled, "Stop, Mr. Scratch is out there!" And the big cat roared with a fury Cord had never heard, or dreamed of hearing.

Mars screamed.

Cord didn't really want to see what Melissa's puma,

driven wild by the gunshots, was doing to the crooked councilman. But he opened the back door and looked outside just for a moment, long enough to see the big cat tearing out great chunks of flesh from a mass of slime and gristle that wasn't dead enough to stop screaming . . .

Cord shut the door. After a while the screams subsided.

He went back to the living room, where the others waited, and sat by Deborah's side. She was crying uncontrollably, crushing her face into a sofa cushion. Cord stroked her hair, thinking that even at her most vulnerable Deborah shared her mother's peculiar charm.

Melissa tightened a bandage on Hop Lee's shoulder, carefully securing it in place. "You've done your job," she told Cord. "The rest is up to the city council. I . . . I'm sorry you had to pay such a price, Cord. I promise you it won't be in vain."

"I know, Melissa." Cord stood up and laid his hand on Deborah's shoulder. "Let's go now, Deborah. I'm taking you home."

Outside, San Francisco was on fire.

At least, it seemed that way to Deborah and Cord as they picked their way through streets gutted by flame and littered with smashed rubble. From their vantage point as they climbed Telegraph Hill, they saw a city tarnished with riots and destruction, under the smoky glow of a hundred blazing buildings. Not even Dante's *Inferno*, thought Cord, could describe the spreading carnage.

"It's unbelievable," said Deborah, staring at the apocalyptic scene. "What's happening down there?"

"Panic," said Cord. "And lots of people frightened of a disease they don't understand."

Deborah shuddered and kept walking. Cord's horse had been lost in all the confusion, so they'd made their way crosstown on foot, carefully skirting the fires and wreckage, avoiding the wild vigilantes. Both were exhausted when they finally reached the familiar Tudor mansion, painted in brown and gray. Cord knocked loudly on the door.

Victoria Meyers opened it suspiciously—at least, until she saw who it was. Then she flung open the door and grabbed Deborah in a crushing, tearful embrace, burying her face in her daughter's shoulder. Deborah held on tightly. They stayed that way for a long time.

Finally, Victoria let go, and she looked at Cord. "You found her. You brought her back to me."

Cord shrugged. "It wasn't so hard, once she decided to cooperate."

"He told me everything, Mom," said Deborah softly. "About you and Eric, and Billy Fallows. You didn't need to keep it secret."

"But I wanted to," Victoria explained. "It's hard, when you lose someone so close. It's not something I like to dwell on."

Deborah nodded solemnly. "I know, Mom. Fergus and I were close, too; we wanted to get married. But this plague—well, it killed him, and nothing can change that now."

Victoria hugged her all over again. "You're all right, that's what matters. Cord, how did you find her?"

"From a chain of clues," Cord explained. "I knew she'd been kidnapped on her way to see Rheingold. I guessed she was being held somewhere, a captive. I just had to find out who did it."

"And I'm grateful," said Deborah. "But you got one part wrong."

"What's that?"

"Well . . . I wasn't kidnapped going to see Fergus. It was later, after I saw him, after I watched him die. I was going home when those Chinamen grabbed me."

Cord frowned. "They kidnapped you *after* you saw Fergus?"

"That's right."

"But that's impossible. You should have been infected, unless—" Cord broke off, as a thought suddenly occurred to him. It was a fantastic idea, one of the wildest he'd ever had, and he would have dismissed it out of hand under ordinary circumstances. But now that he thought of it, it made more and more sense—and explained some things Cord had wondered about since he first arrived in San Francisco.

"Wait, Cord!" cried Victoria, as Cord set off down the hill again. "Where are you going?"

Cord stopped and looked back at her. "I have to check on something, Vicky, something important. And I have to do it right away, alone."

Victoria nodded and said nothing. Cord set off down the broad slope, absently fingering Deborah's revolver. When he got to the bottom of the hill, he headed for the waterfront.

# 23

"The first one to touch this boat," roared Beefeater McGee, "takes a bellyful of lead home tonight!"

"You won't talk so big," someone yelled back, "when you're breathing seawater at the bottom of the bay!"

Someone in the crowd fired at McGee; a bullet whanged off the hull, ricocheted into the darkness. McGee drew his Remington and fired three shots into the mob, sparking an avalanche of return fire. Soon the wharf reeked of gunpowder and thick black smoke.

Cord Diamondback crouched behind a whiskey barrel, wondering how to cross the firing line. Both sides seemed well armed. McGee's men must have loaded up with shells after the confrontation with Murchison, and the Vigilance Committee members were just as prepared. The gun battle could last for hours.

Unless—

"Cast off!" yelled McGee. "Let the bastards have their city! I've other ports to visit!"

Instantly, two of McGee's men raced across the deck, unfastening the tie lines that held the *Aegean* against the wharf. Despite the bullets flying in all directions, the sailors managed to free the clipper and nudge it out into the bay with long poles.

Cord noticed a steam donkey engine beside him on the wharf planks, a device used for loading and unloading cargo. It was hissing and puffing furiously, probably left running after some last-minute restocking of the *Aegean*'s supplies. Beside it was a coal box on wheels. Cord noticed that the wharf was not level but sloped down a bit, away from him.

Cord leaned his shoulder into the coal box, pushing with all his weight, until the wheeled crate trundled forward.

"Hey, look out for that thing!" yelled a whiny voice. Three people jumped out of its way, and a fourth opened fire on it. Cord dove into the coal box as it bumped forward, picking up speed.

"Someone's in there!" said the whiny voice. Shots rang out on both sides, splintering the wooden container. Cord felt something nick his sleeve as a bullet chewed through the wall and just missed him.

Cord glanced over the lip of the box, then ducked back as a bullet sprayed wood chips into his hair. The *Aegean* was gliding farther out, almost beyond reach already. Cord took a deep breath and threw himself out of the coal box.

He hit the sodden planks, rolled onto his feet, and raced forward, zigzagging. Behind him the gunmen went crazy. Cord planted his foot on the edge of the wharf and launched himself out into space, making a wild grab for a length of rope trailing from the clipper's hull.

He caught it—

—and hung there against the hull, a perfect target for the wharf gunmen. Cord hauled himself up the rope, inches at a time, as a fusillade of shells made

Swiss cheese of the clipper's hull. One of the slugs cut a stripe across Cord's side. Desperately, he kept climbing, but he knew he'd never make it; there were too many bullets flying and not enough places to duck.

Then a burst of answering fire from the *Aegean*'s crew men scattered the marauders.

Cord knew he had only seconds before they would resume firing, angrier than ever. But those seconds were all he needed. Climbing frantically, Cord reached the top and rolled over the gunwhale into the protected space beneath it.

Gunfire roared behind him, deafening at first, then softer as the *Aegean* sailed out of range. Cord had just decided it was safe to raise his head when a brawny hand closed over his shoulder.

"Well, I'll be goddamned!" said Beefeater McGee. "You must have wanted to see me pretty bad, to go to all this trouble to get here."

"I need your help," said Cord earnestly. "The crisis isn't over; it's only getting worse. I need a big favor, right away."

"Just ask," said McGee. "You barely caught us, though. We had to sew up the mainsail; some fool came up here and slashed it. Otherwise, we'd have left hours ago."

"Can we talk privately?" asked Cord.

"Sure." McGee barked some hasty orders to his men, then led Cord down the hall into his cabin. He kicked the door shut behind him, then pulled two wineglasses from a wooden cabinet.

"You look like you could use some refreshment," said McGee.

"Actually, I'd rather get down to business—"

"Nonsense." McGee bent to fill one of the glasses from a squat wine keg at the foot of his bed. The second glass he filled from a nearly identical keg beside it. "There's always time for good wine. *Vin de la Montagne*, from the Buena Vista vineyards of the Sonoma Valley. It's good for you, calms the nerves."

Cord put the glass to his lips, tipped it up, set it aside. "Very nice," he said. "But I didn't come here to talk oenology."

"There you go with those words again. I'm kind of an expert on winemaking myself, Cord. I'll bet you didn't know that."

"I know you're an expert on drinking it."

"True enough," said McGee. "But I like to drink the best. I'm a rich man now; I can afford it."

Cord leaned forward and stuck his finger into the captain's chest. "We've got to go to Sacramento, McGee."

"Sacramento?" McGee spilled some wine on his shirt in surprise. "What the hell for?"

"To petition the governor for emergency aid. This is turning into a full-fledged epidemic, McGee. The city is going to need outside help."

"Why not go to the city council?"

"Are you kidding? Half of them are *behind* this thing. Besides, there's no time. With Jennings dead and half the city in an uproar, it could take days to organize a council meeting. We don't have days—we need help *now*."

McGee drained his glass and tossed it out a porthole. "Okay, Cord, we'll do it." He leaned out the door to the cabin and yelled, "Hey, Carstairs!"

"What's on your mind, Captain?" a youngish voice answered.

"Change course, right away. We're going upriver, to Sacramento."

"Sacramento? Uh . . . may I ask why, sir?"

"To see the governor, you damned fool!" McGee slammed the door, shaking his head. "Why else would anyone go—"

"I'm sick," said Cord.

Without another word he fell off his chair onto the deck, clutching his stomach, thrashing and kicking uncontrollably. "Infected," said Cord weakly. "I'm infected . . . having a seizure . . ."

"Take it easy, now," said McGee, crouching beside him. "You'll be all right."

"No . . . it's fatal . . . highly contagious . . . stay away from me . . ."

"Nonsense," said McGee. He swept Cord off the floor, laid him in bed, pulled a blanket over him. "You rest up here, Cord. You'll be just fine in the morning. And I'm going to make damned sure we get to Sacramento."

McGee watched Cord carefully for a moment, then left, closing the door behind him.


Four hours later, Beefeater McGee stood at the *Aegean*'s helm, idly guiding the wheel. Water lapped at the hull below as the clipper sailed the dark river. McGee liked this time best, when the crew was below decks sleeping off a hard day's work, and he stood alone under the stars.

It satisfied him, somehow. He was the captain not only of this ship but of his life, his fortune—and few men could make such a claim. Most were timid, afraid of risk, hidebound by the fear of uncertainty. McGee had rarely found an exception.

Of course, Diamondback was one—or he had been, before this affair ended his life. McGee couldn't change what had happened, but he was sorry about Cord's death. Diamondback was a long-standing friend, and a sorely missed one. But the captain was an optimist, and he was quite certain things would work out otherwise.

McGee bent over and spat into the sea.

"Good evening," said Cord Diamondback.

"What in hell . . . ?" McGee spun around, saw Cord, and relaxed a bit. "Cord! You startled me, range rat. How you feeling?"

"I'm fine," said Cord. He pointed to the navigational compass. "But I noticed we changed course a while back, McGee. In fact, we're heading in the exact opposite direction, back the way we came. Why is that?"

"To get help for you," said McGee. "You looked pretty bad, Cord. I wanted to get you to a doctor soon as I could, and the closest is back in San Francisco."

"I think there's another reason," said Cord.

"What do you mean?"

"You figured I'd be dead by now, so there was no reason to keep heading for Sacramento. You never meant to go there anyway. You wanted to get on with your original plan, the plan Jake Jennings and Heywood Mars died for, the plan Deborah Meyers was kidnapped to conceal. Because Mars wasn't the Master that Nightmare mentioned—you are."

## 24

"I didn't realize you were sick in the head," said McGee. "What kind of crazy lie is that?"

"No lie at all." Cord folded his arms and leaned against a bulkhead. "At first I thought the Master was Heywood Mars, owner of the plague ship. But it didn't sit right, McGee. The Master was someone Nightmare respected, and Mars didn't seem quite up to it."

"And I do."

"Yeah. But it's not just that. Even the way we met was suspicious. You showed up at just the right time to rescue us from those looters, a coincidence I wondered about even then."

"Well, it *was* a coincidence," snapped McGee. "Do you think I went there on purpose?"

"Yes, I do. You arranged it all with the looters beforehand, told them when the steamer would get there, its size, rate of speed, everything. Then, when you thought it was all over, you showed in this boat to claim your bounty—and found a band of survivors instead. Rather than risk exposure, you decided to rescue them, making yourself an instant hero."

"You're loco!" cried McGee. "How do you know I

didn't just run into your ship, on the way to someplace else?"

"Because it doesn't make sense. You had a ton of pepper on board, and you were heading downriver. But pepper isn't grown in the United States, McGee. It comes from the East Indies, Thailand, India, and Singapore. If you were loaded with it, you must have crossed the ocean and come in through San Francisco Bay—so you'd be heading upriver, not down.

"That means you must have turned around, halfway up the Sacramento. And if I had to guess why, I'd say you went on ahead of us, signaled the looters, waited a while, and then came down to pick up the spoils. Am I right?"

McGee's mouth opened, then closed.

"Here's how I figure it," said Cord. "When you talked to me in your cabin, you figured I'd get mixed up in this because of the Meyers girl. So you arranged a second meeting, in that Barbary Coast alleyway. And when you found out I was boarding the plague ship, you saw a chance to stay right on top of the investigation—by being a part of it."

"You're sicker than I realized," said McGee. "You're suffering from delusions!"

"I doubt it," said Cord. "You see, another thing I wondered about was your willingness to board the *Orpheus*, despite the risk of fatal infection. I did it because Vicky's daughter's life was at stake, and Carpenter did it out of medical curiosity—but why did you? You couldn't have cared less about the council's instructions. You had another reason, and an urgent one."

"I did?"

"Yes. You had to make sure Carpenter *didn't* complete his report. You would have killed us both to stop him, but you didn't have to because Jake Jennings sent Nightmare to do the job. Only Carpenter wasn't quite dead when I found him. He said two words before he died. Later I realized those two words explained everything."

"What words?" asked McGee.

"Prussic acid. He was trying to tell me he found it in the bodies."

"What the hell's prussic acid?"

"Hydrogen cyanide," said Cord. "Those men weren't infected, they were poisoned. It was hard to tell, after the rats had been at them for a week—but Carpenter knew, and he died because of it."

"Jesus, Cord, you think I went on board that ship and poisoned those men?"

"Yes, I do. You seemed awfully familiar with the layout—not surprising, since you'd been there a week earlier poisoning the wine barrels. I even know where you got the poison. It's a chemical derivative of a soluble blue dye, the shade known as cyan. The Dragon's Tongue Garment Mill must have had gallons of the stuff."

"I'm getting mad now," said McGee, the veins on his neck throbbing. "No one talks to me like that, not even you."

"Let me finish. Remember those barrels of almonds we found on the *Orpheus*? They were camouflage. You didn't want anyone to notice the smell of cyanide—it smells like bitter almonds—so you stuck those barrels on board to account for it. Nice idea, but there's one problem: you forgot to update the cargo manifest. It doesn't say a word about almonds."

Cord pulled a stack of bound sheets from his pocket. "Yours does, McGee. According to this, the

*Aegean* should be carrying those barrels. You must have transferred them after you planted the poison.''

"All right, Cord." McGee's face was the color of red wine. "One question, before I tear you into stringy pieces—why? Why would I do this? What would I have to gain?"

"Good question," Cord admitted. "And one that almost stopped me. I finally got it, though." He grinned. "With a little help from the late Mr. Jennings."

"Well?"

"Jennings said something, there in his bedroom, that I didn't think about at the time. It was during my faceoff with Ichabod, right about the time you left to tell Heywood Mars that Jennings was going to murder the girl."

"I didn't—"

"He said something funny. He called your scheme 'the phylloxera thing.' You're the expert on winemaking, McGee. You must have heard of phylloxera."

"Of course I've heard of it, Cord. It's a parasitic fungus, deadly to grapevines. A few years back it wiped out the vineyards of Europe, though the vines in America were untouched."

"So far. But you're planning to change that, aren't you, McGee? The glass globe I found in the garment mill was a culture of phylloxera; the leafy residue came from a contaminated grapevine. That's why it was so important to paint a warning on the globe. Phylloxera *is* 'incurable' and 'fatal'—to grapevines, not people.

"I wasn't sick, and you knew it. You thought I was dying because you spiked my wine with the same poison you used in the *Orpheus's* wine barrels. You did it then because someone, maybe the captain, found the stuff in that locker and knew enough to be dangerous. So you killed the whole crew, except for Rheingold and his friends.

"You didn't get them until they reached San Francisco, did you? They weren't sick on that life raft; they were healthy enough to bring it into port against the strong currents of the bay. But once they got there, someone—either Jennings or Mars—heard about it and went to meet them. And he gave them a nice cool drink, filled with the same poison they'd missed on the *Orpheus*. By the time Deborah got there they were already dying, just like their crewmates—and just like me, if I'd drunk your wine instead of only pretending to."

"Quite a story," said McGee. "But you still haven't told me what I get out of it."

Cord spread his hands. "The answer is simple. You've developed an unstoppable strain of phylloxera, using the selective breeding techniques suggested by Darwin and developed by Mendel. And you're going to use it to wipe out all the vineyards in the United States and Europe—except, of course, your own.

"Wine prices will skyrocket. You'll be rich, rich beyond imagining. And no one will ever guess the connection between your vast fortune and the plague scare that destroyed half of San Francisco."

McGee laughed. It came from nowhere, a big, bellowing laugh that shook his belly and sent a tremor through the deck. For half a minute he laughed. Then he sobered and looked squarely at Cord.

"You really are something, Diamondback. You figured it all out, the whole thing, right down to the vineyards I've got in Australia and the money I'll make from the wine shortage. Very clever, Cord."

He sighed. "Of course, this means I'll have to kill

you before I turn you in for the reward on Christopher Deacon. I can't have you repeating any of this. Still"
—he offered a smile—"it's damned impressive."

McGee pulled a cord and a deafening whistle split the air. "Everyone on deck," he roared. "I got someone up here needs killing—and ten pounds of gold for the first man to do it!"

# 25

No one came. No one at all. The deck was empty except for Cord, and a very puzzled McGee.

"There's something I forgot to tell you," Cord confessed. "I found the poison bottle you used to doctor the *Orpheus*'s wine barrels. I got even by poisoning yours. Any of your crew who had a drink before bedtime—most all of them, I expect—are suffering from cyanide poisoning. Just like the crew of the *Orpheus*."

"You poisoned my crew?" gasped McGee.

"With a bottle I found in your cabin. I figured I was giving them a fair chance, McGee. If I was wrong, your crew would be fine. If I was right—well, piracy is a capital offense. So's murder, or conspiracy to commit murder. There I go, playing judge again."

McGee looked frantically at the hallway leading to the crew's quarters, but it showed no signs of life. He gave the whistle another blast, and roared at the top of his lungs, like a lion in a pit—but no one answered his summons. Finally, he squared his shoulders and turned to face Cord.

"Well, old buddy, guess I'll have to kill you myself."

"You can try," said Cord.

McGee lunged forward, grabbing for Cord's throat. Cord sidestepped him and threw a jab into McGee's kidneys. McGee didn't seem to feel it, but Cord's hand hurt from the impact.

"You gonna fight, or dance around?" snapped McGee. He threw a left at Cord's jaw with most of his weight behind it. Cord ducked the blow but felt it go by, like the wash of air after a racing locomotive. Cord threw a stomach punch, hard, and followed it with an uppercut at McGee's lantern jaw. McGee shrugged off both blows and grabbed Cord's wrist in a bruising, unbreakable grip.

"Got you!" McGee bellowed. The captain swung Cord by the arm and smashed him into the side of the wheelhouse, shattering one of the windows. He yanked Cord back again, tightening his grip, and backhanded him with a Bunyon-sized hand. Cord reeled away but couldn't duck the next one because of McGee's lockhold on his wrist.

Then a meat-hook fist sailed into his forehead and Cord felt the world go soft around the edges, like the slush at the edge of a snowdrift. Cord tried to swing with his free hand, but McGee easily batted it aside and drove his kunckles into Cord's mouth. Cord tasted salt, and felt a warm stickiness over his chin.

McGee slammed him into the wall again. He slapped Cord, pounded the side of his head, hit him in the ribs, and felt something crack. Cord went limp, head lolling to one side. McGee reached for Cord's throat to snap it like a chicken bone.

Cord hit him.

Not with his free hand, McGee was ready for that. Cord used his other hand, still encircled at the wrist, gambling on the captain's sluggish reflexes to keep him from diverting the punch. Cord felt the captain's nose bend and break under his knuckles. McGee howled in pain and let Cord go, clutching his face with both hands.

Cord hit him in the stomach with his left hand, then his right, then his left again. McGee grunted and backed off a step, balling his fists. Cord feinted left, lunged right, and hit McGee's nose again, even harder. McGee screamed in rage and pain and charged Cord, clawing at his face. Cord waited a beat, then dove aside as McGee crashed headlong into the navigator's wheel.

"Bastard, I'll kill you!" roared the captain. He took the wheel in both hands and tore it free of its brass fittings, buckling and splintering the polished oak. The wheel snapped free of its moorings and McGee raised it over his head, coming forward, trying to smash Cord like a waterbug under its hard weight.

Cord ran. He left the wheelhouse, darted into the interior hallway. McGee blundered after him, holding tight to the wheel. The captain reached the hallway and was knocked off his feet when the wheel jammed against both side walls, too broad to fit between them. McGee cast it aside and went on after Diamondback, holding one hand to his nose.

The door to McGee's cabin was open. McGee stepped inside and yelled as a barrel full of California wine came down on his skull. He struck out blindly with his right hand, caught Diamondback on the breastbone, and smacked him clean across the cabin. Cord sprawled against McGee's giant bed, wincing at the pain from his injured rib.

McGee rubbed his neck, fighting dizziness. He lurched forward and Cord kicked the side of his knee, toppling him onto the deck. Cord rolled out of reach and fetched up against a bulkhead, holding his side.

"You never could lick me in a fight, Cord," said McGee, hoisting himself upright.

"I was never fool enough to keep fighting," said Cord. "At least, not until now."

"Hell, give it up, Cord. I'll make it fast; you'll hardly know what happened. Think of it as a favor, a gift from an old friend."

Cord met his eyes. "Not this time, McGee."

"Yeah, that's what I figured." McGee threw open a nearby steamer trunk and pulled out a rapier, in a hand-tooled scabbard. "Okay, Chris—forget this Cord Diamondback bullshit—I'm going to slice you up into whale bait."

McGee rushed forward, thrusting and slashing. Cord threw a wad of linen at him and McGee sliced it clean in half, then quartered it on the return slash. Cord dove over the foot of the bed as McGee slashed again and took a chunk out of the footboard.

McGee lumbered forward, hacking at the air. Cord backed away, running out of dodging space. McGee braced himself, jumped forward, and brought the rapier down where Cord used to be, over one of the wine barrels. The rapier carved a slice out of the barrel and stuck there, embedded in the wood.

"Damn it!" roared McGee, grasping the hilt with both hands. He pulled hard and the rapier came free, tearing the top of the barrel off with it. McGee was turning around when Cord launched himself off the bed and landed square on the captain's shoulders, knocking him off his feet.

McGee fell to his knees. Cord's arms went under his shoulders and back around his neck, in a crushing full nelson. McGee tried to throw him off but Diamondback forced him down, dousing McGee's head in the open barrel of wine. McGee lurched and heaved under Cord's wrestling grip, trying to get his head out, trying to breathe.

Cord might have drowned him, if he'd been uninjured. But his rib was broken, and his arm was bleeding again, and when McGee made one last heave Cord lost his grip and fell harmlessly away. McGee wiped his mouth, coughing and spluttering, spitting out wine and saliva.

"Thought you could . . . drown me . . . huh, Chris?" McGee rubbed his throat, breathing fitfully. "Too bad . . . couldn't hold me . . . your last chance . . ."

"Wrong again," said Cord. "It's all over, McGee. That was the wine you poisoned, remember? You must have swallowed a quart of it in the fight. You're a dead man, old friend."

McGee paled. He turned to look at the barrel, eyes widening in fear, and Cord snatched up his rapier and rammed it full force into the hollow of McGee's throat. The captain made a strangled, wheezing sound, clawing at the blade with both hands. He fell on his side, still grasping the blade, blood puddling under his shoulders.

"My mistake," said Cord. "The other barrel was poisoned, not this one."

McGee's great frame shuddered twice, and was still. Cord staggered to the door, holding his side, going out to revive himself in the cool night air.

But the door was blocked by a black-clad figure.

"Good evening, Diamondback," said Nightmare cordially. "I knew we'd meet again. I have a special death for you, a death of my own invention. I hope you appreciate this honor."

# 26

"Shall I explain how you're going to die?" asked Nightmare.

Cord shrugged. "Sure, go ahead."

"Very well. I'm going to embed two fingernails of my right hand in your eyes, Diamondback. A strike to the eyes with sufficient force can penetrate to the brain, but mine will not; I will enter your eyes and go no farther, as long as you do not move. The length of your lifetime will be the number of minutes you can remain completely immobile."

Nightmare smiled behind the mask. "One further detail. As you stand there, blinded and paralyzed, I will shred the skin from your body with the fingernails of my left hand."

"Suppose I don't want to play?"

"Ah, but you must," Nightmare insisted. "I am quite capable of forcing you. You see, Diamondback, even at your best you were not my match. In your injured, exhausted condition, you cannot oppose me."

Cord hit him in the stomach. Nightmare reeled back, unhurt but astonished at the blow. "You fool! Are your actions untempered by reason? Don't you realize the consequences of my anger?"

Cord hit him again, or tried to, but Nightmare

leaned away from the blow and smashed the heel of his hand into Cord's face. Cord stumbled backward as Nightmare sent a lift kick to his groin and threw an elbow smash across Cord's cheek. Cord tripped over McGee's body and sprawled across the floor.

"Now stand before me," said Nightmare, "and die."

"Sure you wouldn't like some of McGee's wine first?"

Nightmare kicked the broken barrel, a precise blow that shattered it instantly and drenched the deck with wine. "No more games, Diamondback. I am waiting."

"All right." Cord grabbed a stave from the barrel and snapped it in two, leaving a jagged, broken edge. He stood up and moved close to Nightmare, holding the rough-edged halves in either hand.

Nightmare threw a hook kick at his stomach. Cord struck at his leg with the barrel stave, giving him splinters but nothing else. Nightmare followed with a backhand punch and a side kick that knocked one of the barrel staves out of Cord's hand.

Cord dove for him with the other stave. Nightmare glided away. Cord's attack tore a shred of silk from his enemy's costume but left him off balance for Nightmare's rejoinder, an elbow thrust to the face. Cord fell back, stunned, and sat down hard on the deck.

Nightmare came forward, hands massaging the air. Cord got up again and lunged at him, brandishing the stave. Nightmare caught his sleeve and threw him across the room onto the deck planks. Cord landed next to McGee's rapier, as he'd planned; he grabbed it and took a broad swipe at Nightmare, drawing blood from the Chinaman's chest.

Startled, Nightmare faded back into the doorway.

Cord shifted his grip on the rapier and went after him. He ducked through the doorway, holding the blade steady, wary of an ambush, but Nightmare was gone.

Cord pressed forward. At the end of the hallway the passage was blocked by the navigator's wheel, still jammed against the opening where McGee had left it. Gingerly, Cord stepped over it and was taken by surprise when Nightmare drove four steel-tipped fingernails into the muscles of his chest.

Cord twisted away, trying to keep Nightmare's fingers from the soft tissues of his throat. He brought the rapier blade up to skewer Nightmare's hand, but the Oriental killer was already out of reach, staying tauntingly outside the striking range of Cord's blade.

Nausea swept over Diamondback. He was bleeding from the arm and chest, and he had a persistent headache—probably a residual effect of the concussion he'd suffered at the Jennings mansion. He had to finish Nightmare quickly, or not at all.

"You're weakening," said Nightmare, in a tone of genuine amusement. "I predicted you could not fight me in your injured condition. Surrender to me now, Diamondback, and accept your sad defeat."

Cord swung the rapier, coming nowhere near him. Nightmare laughed and stepped closer. Cord took another swing, off target just as badly, and Nightmare darted in to stab at Cord's eyes, but it was just what Cord expected. He brought the rapier up harder and faster than ever before and sliced off Nightmare's hand.

Nightmare shrieked and scrambled away, his stump spurting blood like a firehose. Clumsily, Cord pursued him. Nightmare tore a strip of black silk from his garment and bound his wrist to staunch the bleeding. Cord raised the rapier to behead him and Nightmare surprised him with a spinning back kick that knocked the blade out of Cord's hands and into the sea.

"I am . . . not whole," said Nightmare numbly. "I cannot . . . cannot live like this." He looked at Cord with coldly dawning rage. "You . . . did this to me . . . you must . . . pay price . . ."

Cord retreated, casting about for a weapon. Perhaps he could wait until Nightmare passed out from sheer blood loss—however long it took. But the man seemed so unstoppable Cord could half believe he *was* protected by Satan, a demon who walked like a man.

Then, suddenly, Cord found a weapon. He bent to get it and Nightmare sprang at him, swinging the stump of his right hand, side-kicking with the opposite leg. Cord took a vicious blow to the kidneys and flopped onto the deck, gasping in pain. Nightmare kicked at him again and again, all reason forgotten in his fervor for destruction.

But Cord was suffering on purpose.

He hunched into a ball, feigning anguish, trying to draw his quarry closer. Nightmare approached him, swearing profusely. Cord waited for him to get too close, then reached up and grabbed a handful of silk from Nightmare's torn costume.

Nightmare tried to pull free, but Cord lashed out with his newfound weapon: Nightmare's severed hand. Cord dug the reinforced fingernails into the pulsing artery at the Chinaman's armpit. Nightmare screamed and tried to hold the wound closed, but he'd lost too much blood already.

He swore, then crashed to the ground. After a while he stopped breathing.

Cord left him there and made his way to the cargo hold, carrying a kerosene lantern. The *Aegean*'s cargo, he knew, included a deadly fungus that could cripple one of California's most lucrative industries. It mustn't be allowed to leave this ship, ever.

Cord examined the hold. The inside hull was a mottled gray, and slippery to the touch. The walls here, he realized, had been soaked with flammable oils, probably from tons of whale blubber over a period of years. The whole ship was a floating firetrap. He returned to the deck and saw the lights of San Francisco flickering in the distance.

Cord lowered the *Aegean*'s small lifeboat into the water and cut it loose. Then he pitched the lantern into the cargo hold and jumped into the water. As he swam to the lifeboat and climbed inside it, Cord could feel the heat of the clipper burning behind him. It felt good against his sodden clothing.

Best of all, though, was the fact that his guess had been right. The plague was a hoax; he could tell the *Examiner* there was no disease to conquer, no epidemic to deal with. The panic would be over, with no further damage and minimal loss of life.

Cord raised the sail of the small lifeboat, and guided his craft toward shore.

# 27

"It's really over now?" asked Victoria Meyers.

Cord nodded wearily. They were sitting on the couch, under the sweeping bay window in the living room of Victoria's home. Victoria had fussed over Cord's injuries for the better part of an hour, after he'd dragged himself to her doorstep and collapsed there. She'd shaken her head, marveling that he was still alive after all he'd suffered in the previous hours.

"And how did you ever get the lifeboat back into the harbor, Cord? It's a miracle you were even conscious, let alone able to manage a boat."

Cord touched her fondly on the chin. "I was motivated," he explained.

Victoria smiled, and the phantom charm Cord loved so much had never been more abundant. "Looks like I owe you one, Cord."

"Don't mention it, Vicky." He sat back, admiring her smile. "How's Deborah taking all this?"

"As well as you'd expect. She adored Billy Fallows—same as everyone—and I never bothered to tell her different. So it'll be a while before she can accept everything you told her. But Melissa can help. She knew Fallows best of all—and she has nothing kind to say about him. That more than anything should bring Deborah around.''

"I'm glad," Cord said sincerely.

Victoria rested her hand on his shoulder, on the side that wasn't wounded. "Thank you, Cord," she said softly. "I know what you were risking, even to come here—but I wasn't surprised when you did. You haven't changed a bit, have you?" she said, raising her head and looking him in the eye.

"Maybe some," Cord allowed. "I'm . . . at peace now, Vicky, more than ever before. I love the work of judging, the constant test of wits. I wouldn't have been happy doing anything but this."

"That's our problem, isn't it, Cord?" Victoria rested her head on his unwounded shoulder. "I couldn't do what you do. I need civilization, the trappings of law and order—a system to work inside. I need rules, I guess, and half the jobs you get don't have any. I don't know how you do it."

"Wisdom and training," said Cord.

"And a bit of the old blarney, right?" Impulsively, she kissed him. "Listen, Cord, how long before you have to saddle up and get out of here?"

"Well, I should leave as soon as possible," Cord said slowly. "Of course, it'd be unwise to travel before my wounds are properly healed. And that could take quite a while."

Victoria gave him a dazzling smile. "The longer the better, Cord."

*Watch for*

## THE SECRET OF MORRO ROCK

next in the Diamondback series
from Pinnacle Books

*coming in February!*